MURDER AT MINSTREL MANOR

ROBERT WENSON

For my Mother

CONTENTS

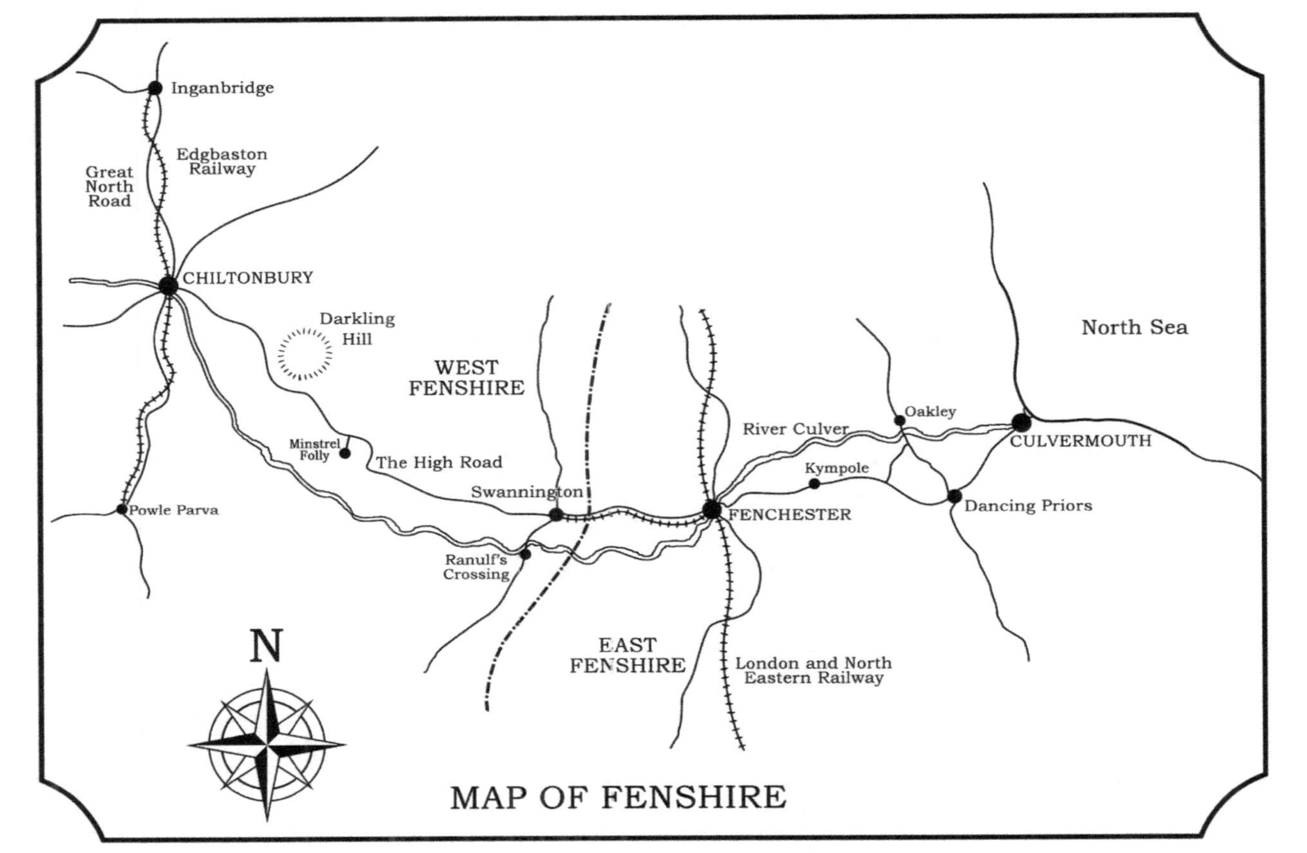

MAP OF FENSHIRE

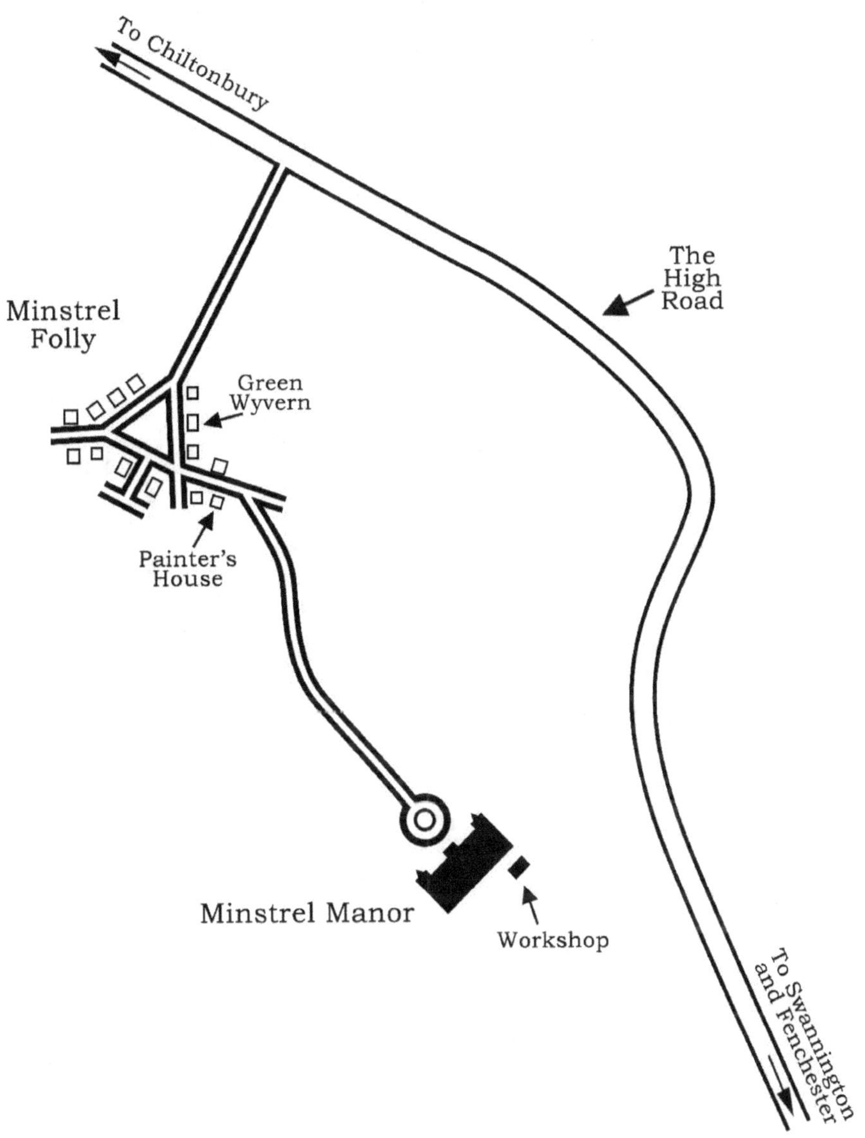

MINSTREL MANOR & MINSTREL FOLLY

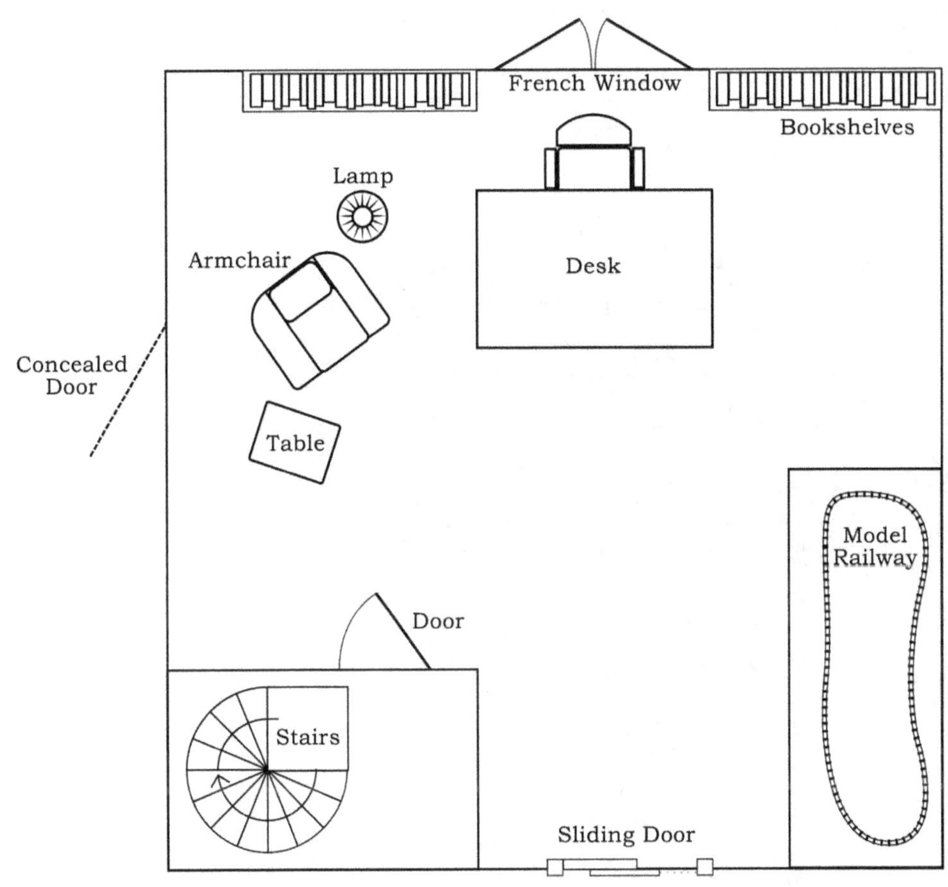

Plan of Study

KILLED? AS IN MURDERED?

A winter storm raged in the night outside Minstrel Manor. Within, the ponderous and rhythmic ticking of a long-case clock opposed the irregular whistling and roaring of the storm. At three minutes to ten o'clock, Pembert the butler, a man rather under middle height whose grey hair and lined face made him look far older than his forty-seven years, came up the passage. He carried a silver tray bearing a bottle of whisky, a soda-water syphon, and an empty glass. Setting the tray on a small table beside the clock, he knocked at what appeared to be a plain panel in the wall.

As the clock began to sound its ten strokes, Pembert frowned and knocked again. After a few moments he pressed at a particular spot in the moulding framing the panel. A piece of the moulding swung outward to reveal a small white button with a slot beneath. He took a small strip of metal from his pocket, inserted it into the slot and turned it anti-clockwise, then pressed the button. The door slid open, revealing the study of Sebastian Oldfield, owner of Minstrel Manor, well-known as a scientist, inventor, and recluse. Pembert picked up the tray and entered the study.

A few minutes later he came out, pale and agitated. He stood irresolute for a moment; then, collecting himself, the butler hastened back down the passage to another, ordinary door that was ajar. Through this door he entered the library, where he picked up the telephone and asked to be put through to the police station in Minstrel Folly.

"I say, Pembert, what's the matter?" These words were spoken by a young woman curled up in an armchair with *War and Peace*.

Before the butler could answer, a voice on the telephone informed him that Constable Higgins was on the other end and wished to know the reason for the call.

"I am calling from Minstrel Manor... Yes, this is Pembert. Mr. Oldfield has been killed. For God's sake, come at once!" Pembert turned to the young woman to apologise for inflicting such alarming news upon her without warning. "I beg your pardon, Miss Hackett —" he began.

"Killed!" cried Edwina Hackett. "Really? As in murdered?"

"It appears so," replied the butler.

"Tell me about it!" said Edwina, her hazel eyes sparkling with excitement.

"Mr. Oldfield has been killed in his study. That is all I know."

The butler's careworn face, Edwina observed, was quivering with emotion. "Oh — that was thoughtless of me, wasn't it," she said. "I *am* sorry."

"Thank you, Miss Hackett," said Pembert. "It is a great shock."

"Were you — was he a good master? I hadn't got to know him very well."

"Yes, he was. We shall miss him very much... Please excuse me — I don't like it that he's sitting there all alone. I must go back to him until the constable arrives."

"I'll come with you," declared Edwina, setting aside *War and Peace*.

Pembert remained outside the study, but Edwina, irrepressibly curious, entered at once, intending to observe all she could. Her eyes were at once attracted to the desk, opposite the door, over which Sebastian Oldfield's body slumped. She approached the desk. The dreadful wound in Oldfield's head, and the reddish-brown stains on the bronze dragon which served as a paperweight, made it clear how he had been killed. His head and upper body rested on the desk. His left arm was stretched out towards a telephone; beneath his right hand was a drawing-pencil.

Oldfield had dined in his study. On the desk lay the remains of his meal: a plate bearing pieces of cracked lobster shell, a stalk of asparagus, and some fragments of bread, and beside it a half-empty bottle of Burgundy. Edwina, a painter by profession, could not help putting a title to it: *Still Life with Corpse.*

A small silver bowl lay on its side beside a puddle of butter and an overturned wineglass. Oldfield's left arm lay partly in the puddle — Edwina presumed he had overturned the bowl and glass while groping for the telephone. Some of the wine had spilled and left a reddish residue; she touched it and found it slightly sticky. The spirit-lamp that had kept the butter melted had rolled off the desk. The carpet beneath it was unscorched; Edwina concluded that the lamp had been extinguished in the fall.

Beside the telephone was a vertical row of small white buttons. Edwina wondered what they were for, but left them alone; not only because she knew one mustn't touch anything, but her father, a machinist, had drilled into her that one doesn't press a button unless one is SURE what it does.

Edwina turned her attention to the study itself. It was a squarish room, lit by two fixtures hanging from the ceiling. The walls were paneled in dark wood and the floor carpeted in crimson. Behind the desk was a French window, partially obscured by heavy drapes of the same colour as the carpet. On either side of the window stood tall bookcases.

To the left the study extended into a shallow alcove, containing a comfortable armchair flanked by a standard lamp and a small, low table. On the table were stacked four or five magazines and, on top of them, a book. Someone had been using it as a convenient platform for drinks, judging by the rings which stained it. Beside this pile was a small sheet of sketch paper upon which Edwina was surprised to find a vivid but not unkind caricature of herself.

In the side wall of the alcove was an ordinary wooden door; several cardboard boxes, labeled "Hornby," were piled in front of it.

The end wall bore several framed prints. Edwina went to examine them more closely. They portrayed theatrical scenes: some she recognised at once as being from Shakespeare; the others, she judged by the costumes and actions, were from nineteenth-century melodramas.

The only other furnishing of the study was a long table running along the wall opposite the alcove. It bore an elaborate and minutely detailed model railway and surrounding countryside. Midway along the table were the controls of the trains: toggles, switches, and vari-coloured lights. Before them was a tall stool for the operator.

Remembering just in time to wrap a handkerchief around her hand so as not to leave fingerprints, Edwina tried both the French window and the door in the alcove and found both locked.

Unwilling to abandon Pembert to a solitary vigil until the constable arrived, she fetched *War and Peace* from the library and settled down, uncomfortably, on the wooden floor of the passage.

The clock struck the half-hour; then the three-quarters. "Shouldn't the constable be here by now?" remarked Edwina. "It's only about a fifteen-minute walk between the village and the manor."

"He must have been delayed by the storm," said Pembert. Edwina returned to her book.

Finally, however, there came the sound of a distant knocking, followed some moments later by a crash — the wind had caught the front door as soon as it was opened and flung it wide. Then, a murmur of voices. And finally, escorted by William the footman, Constable Higgins, large, blue-eyed, his normally pink cheeks reddened by the winter wind, appeared at the far end of the passage. Flecks and patches of snow still clung to the helmet he carried, his boots, and the legs of his trousers, which were soaked to the knees. Pembert and Edwina, who had arisen as soon as she heard the door, and was now unobtrusively wriggling to unstiffen herself, stood waiting.

Constable Higgins began to set down his helmet on the table beside the clock, noticed the wet snow upon it, and put it down on the floor instead. As he was taking out his notebook and pencil, the youthful William forgot the decorum of a servant long enough to lean sideways and look past Pembert into the study. Turning slightly green, he began to sidle off.

Pembert pulled him up short. "I did not tell you to go, William," he snapped. The footman at once stopped and came to attention. Unwilling to have William present during the interview with Constable Higgins, but also feeling it was *his* duty as the butler to inform the staff of the untoward events of the evening, he instructed the footman to wait in the library, which William was only too glad to do.

When William had departed, Higgins opened his notebook. Turning to a fresh page, he wrote at the head, *Investigation of report of murder at Minstrel Manor — 18 January, 1927 (Monday)*. The clock struck the hour and he added, *11:00 PM*.

"If you will be so good as to wait here," he said, "I shall examine the scene of the alleged crime."

Pembert stood aside and Higgins entered the study. Going to the desk, he looked closely at the body and the paperweight. Then, as Edwina had done, he subjected the room to a careful scrutiny, pausing now and then to write in his notebook. Pembert and Edwina remained in the passage, the former waiting impassively save for an impatient tapping of his foot, the latter observing Higgins with the same interest as she had shown earlier during her own investigation of the study.

Finally Higgins emerged. "It appears murder has indeed been

done," he announced. Pembert snorted. Ignoring this, the constable asked, "I must report this to police headquarters in Fenchester. Is there a telephone I can use?"

"There's one right there in the study," said Pembert.

"He can't use that one," said Edwina. "One mustn't touch anything at the scene of the crime. Isn't that right, constable — er —"

"Higgins, Miss. And you are correct."

"There's one in the library."

"All the telephones in this house are Mr. Oldfield's invention," interjected Pembert. "I shall come with you and show you how to call outside."

"Thank you, Mr. Pembert," said Higgins. "Please accompany us, Miss Hackett. I mustn't leave anyone alone at the scene of the crime."

The three went to the library and Higgins called police head-quarters.

"This is Police Constable Higgins, stationed in Minstrel Folly," he began when he had been put through. "I wish to report that a murder has been committed at Minstrel Manor... The victim is Sebastian Oldfield, the owner. I am calling from the manor... Some time this evening... Just beyond Minstrel Folly — you go directly through the village and there is the drive up to the manor... Yes, Sergeant, I shall wait here."

At Police Headquarters, Sergeant Guntram carefully noted the call in the log. Then he called Superintendent Runciman, apologised for the lateness of the call, and relayed the report.

The Superintendent looked out of his window at the flying snow and considered. Finally he made up his mind. George Mallow — young, zealous, recently promoted to Detective-Inspector: time to give him some real experience.

Detective-Inspector Mallow was awakened from a sound sleep by his Superintendent's call.

"George!" came Runciman's voice. "I have a policeman's dream for you."

"Sir?" replied Mallow, warily, groping for his spectacles. He was familiar with his chief's sense of humour.

"I'm giving you a murder to investigate. A real English country-house murder."

"One footman killing another over the affections of a housemaid?"

"Oh, *much* better: the owner of Minstrel Manor."

"Where is that?"

"If you're going to succeed in your career, my boy, you'll have to learn Fenshire by heart. It's just beyond Minstrel Folly. You know where *that* is, don't you?"

"Yes, sir. But Minstrel Folly is in *West* Fenshire. Shouldn't it be a job for the Chiltonbury force?"

"You'd think so, wouldn't you? But somehow — a quirk of old manorial law or something, I never could get the rights of it — Minstrel Folly is part of East Fenshire."

"I see. That is, I don't see, but I'll take your word for it."

"Go to it, George. I know it's an ungodly hour, but murderers have no consideration for us poor coppers. Give me a report as soon as you can."

"Yes, sir."

"Don't forget to lay on an inquest. The coroner is Henry Radford. He's a solicitor — works in Swannington."

"Yes, sir."

Mallow looked at the clock and then out the window. For all his zeal, he was none too pleased to be informed late at night that he had been assigned to a case of murder, separated from him by miles of winter storm; nevertheless, duty was duty. He called headquarters.

"Sergeant Guntram? This is Inspector Mallow."

"Yes, sir?"

"I'll be going to Minstrel Folly. It's a murder case. Get Sergeants Bellman, Henley, and Vanderleun and a couple of constables to meet me at headquarters. We'll need Dr. Melmoth, too. Lay on two cars and the mortuary van." Mallow looked at the clock and out the window again. "And some flasks of hot coffee."

"Is there anything else, Higgins?" asked Pembert when the constable had hung up.

"I must ask some questions," said Higgins. "The inspector will be wanting a full report. Now, who found the body?"

"I did," replied Pembert.

Higgins wrote *Interview with Arthur Pembert (butler), Minstrel Manor.* "If you will be so good as to remain here, Miss," he said to Edwina, "I shall speak with Mr. Pembert in the passage."

"Oh, please, stay here," replied Edwina. "I've always wanted to see a murder investigation first-hand. I'd hate to miss the opportunity."

Higgins, mildly shocked at her levity, was inclined to object; but he sensed this young woman would not heed a mere village constable. "Very well, Miss," he said. He turned to Pembert.

"At what time did you find Mr. Oldfield?"

"It would have been just after ten o'clock."

"And how did you come to enter the study?"

"I was bringing Mr. Oldfield a whisky-and-soda, as I always do at ten."

Higgins transferred his attention to Edwina. "And you, Miss. May I have your name and address, please?"

"Edwina Victoria Hackett, Trafalgar Cottage, Kympole, Fenshire," answered Edwina briskly.

"Thank you. Can you tell me anything about the crime?"

"I can corroborate — I think that's the right word — what Pembert just told you. I saw him come by with a tray — I was in the library — just before ten. I heard —"

Higgins held up his hand. "Excuse me, Miss, while I write this down... How did you know the time?"

"The clock struck ten. Just before it struck I heard Pembert knocking on the door."

"I see."

"It's as Miss Hackett said," put in Pembert. "Mr. Oldfield didn't open the door. I knocked again, then opened it myself and went into the study."

"Was this his custom, Mr. Pembert?" As far as Higgins knew, well-trained servants only knocked before entering a bedroom, and opened doors themselves.

"Yes. When I went into the study, I saw at once something had happened to Mr. Oldfield. I set down the tray and went to him immediately to see if he had taken ill, or needed assistance. Then I saw his head —" Pembert stopped.

"Thank you, Mr. Pembert, you needn't go into that now," said Higgins. "I think the inspector will wish to hear the details himself. And then you called to report the murder?"

"It took me a few minutes to compose myself," said Pembert. "Then I went to the library and rung up the station."

"Do you know at what time Mr. Oldfield entered the study?"

"No. However, he invariably dined there at 7 o'clock, unless there were guests. William brought him his dinner; he can say whether or not Mr. Oldfield was there. I should add that the master insisted upon being left alone and undisturbed between seven and ten."

William, summoned from the library, informed Higgins that Mr. Oldfield had been in the study at seven.

"Very well, Mr. Pembert, I think that will be all for now," said Higgins. "And now, Miss," he addressed Edwina, "can you tell me anything more?"

"I was in the library when Pembert came in to ring up the station," said Edwina. "Afterwards, he wished to return to Mr. Oldfield. I decided to go with him."

"And why was that?" asked Higgins, again mildly shocked — but now, not surprised — that this apparently well-bred young woman would voluntarily go to the scene of a violent crime.

"As I said earlier, I've always wanted to see a murder investigation up close. When we got there, Pembert waited outside the study. I went in and looked about, but apart from the body itself, and the murder weapon, I didn't see anything that looked like a clue; but of course, I'm not a policeman. I'm sure you saw all sorts of clues."

In fact, Higgins had not (as far as he knew), but he refrained from saying this. He was forced to accept that not only had this young lady gone to the scene, but she had calmly entered the room and examined the body. "Did you disturb anything in the room?" he asked.

"No."

Higgins wrote all this down. He considered adding a parenthetical remark about Edwina's unnaturally composed attitude toward the murder, but decided the Inspector could come to his own conclusions.

"Oh!" exclaimed Edwina. "I just realised — the murderer must have come and gone through the other door, or the window."

"Why do you say that, Miss?"

"Nobody came along the passage between seven and ten."

"How do you know that?"

"I was in a chair facing the library door and the door was open. I'm a bit claustrophobic; I don't like being in a closed room."

"Could you have dozed?"

"No. I never doze."

"Very well then. I must wait here until the inspector arrives from Fenchester. They told me the roads were so bad on account of the storm, he won't be here for quite some time. It mayn't be my place to say so, but I suggest you all go to bed."

"Quite," said Pembert. He and William turned to go.

Edwina, however, demurred. "Certainly not," she declared. "For one thing, I shan't sleep a wink, and for another, I want very much to meet this inspector. If it's all right, I'll stay in the library. But if you'll excuse me for just a moment —" She left to visit the cloakroom.

"Mr. Pembert," said Higgins. "How can I close the door to the study?"

"I'll show you," replied the butler. He took the constable to the door. "Pay attention, now." He turned the key back and removed it and the panel closed. "The door will not open without the key," he said. "To open the door, turn the key and press the button. Turn the key clockwise and the door closes thirty seconds after it has been opened; turn it anti-clockwise to open the door and leave it open."

"How strange. May I see the key?" Pembert handed it over. "I've never seen anything like it."

"It's magnetic — I think. The door is another one of Mr. Oldfield's inventions."

"Perhaps you'll allow me to keep the key, Mr. Pembert, and I shall give it to the inspector."

"Mr. Oldfield gave strict instructions — I don't suppose it matters, now." Accompanied by William, the butler retired to the servants' quarters. Higgins remained at the study door.

Edwina returned. "I hope the inspector won't take too long," she said to Higgins. "But with this weather..." She went into the library and settled down with *War and Peace.*

Higgins kept vigil, listening to the ticking of the clock and the raging storm outside. From time to time, when his legs had grown restive with standing, he strolled down the passage and back, glancing into the library each time. The first time, Edwina waved to him; the second, he saw her curled up in her armchair, fast asleep. He tactfully closed the library door.

Just after one o'clock, the storm died away, and only the ticking of the clock broke the silence.

2

THE POLICE FROM FENCHESTER

At two o'clock, a brace of police cars slowly made their way up the snow-blanketed drive, followed by a mortuary van, and stopped in front of the manor. From the leading car emerged Detective-Inspector Mallow.

The storm had passed away and the westering moon, just at the full, shone brilliantly in a cloudless sky. Minstrel Manor was a solid and sober house, plain but elegant. A tracery of vines, leafless in winter, wandered over the brick façade. The main block was flanked on either side by wings, perceptibly of recent date, but in keeping with the original character of the manor.

Mallow went up to the pedimented door and gave it several brisk raps with the knocker. Some minutes later the door opened and William the footman, somewhat bleary-eyed and rumpled, looked out.

"Good evening — or, rather, good morning," said the inspector. "I hope this is Minstrel Manor?"

"Yes, sir," said William. "Are you the police from Fenchester?"

"Yes." Mallow introduced himself. "Please wait a moment while I fetch my men."

The inspector went back to the waiting vehicles and returned with his colleagues: square and grizzled Bellman; tall, broad-shouldered Henley, the fingerprint expert; middle-sized, stout Vanderleun, bearing his photographic equipment; and two constables, placid Porlock and eager Pyke. Behind them, accompanied by two men from the mortuary van bearing a stretcher, was the police surgeon, Dr. Melmoth, bleary-eyed and annoyed at being called out at such an unGodly hour.

"Now," Mallow addressed William, "please take me to Constable Higgins."

"This way, sir," said William, and Mallow found himself in the hall of Minstrel Manor.

The manor had begun life as a handsome Georgian building and had survived the Victorian era untouched. Since its purchase by Sebastian Oldfield, however, it had been altered by the addition of the two wings. The wing in which the study was located (on the left hand if one was facing the house) also included a new library. The old library and the entrance hall had been thrown together, forming a social space instead of a mere thoroughfare. As William conducted him across the hall, Mallow made a quick mental inventory of its contents: several overstuffed armchairs; a sofa against one wall and a set of six gilt chairs divided in pairs against the others; a long table bearing a number of newspapers; a writing-desk; and, between two windows, an intricate wood-and-brass affair combining a clock, a barometer, and gauges to display the inside and outside temperatures and the speed and direction of the wind. There was no carpet, for which Mallow, conscious of the snow on his boots, was grateful.

William escorted Mallow up the passage from the hall to where Higgins stood vigil.

"Ah — Constable Higgins," said Mallow. "I'm sorry you had to wait so long — the roads are dreadful."

"That's all right, sir," replied Higgins.

"Where's the body?" asked Mallow. He gestured down the passage to the library door. "In there?"

"No, sir," said Higgins. He gave Pembert's key to Mallow and explained how it worked. Mallow tried it, first clockwise and then anti-clockwise. "How odd," he said. "We'll leave it open for now." He entered the study and skimmed his eyes over Oldfield's body and the furnishings of the room. "Wait here while I get my men. Then I'll hear your report."

"Yes, sir," said Higgins, saluting.

The specialists set to work. Sergeant Henley, assisted by Porlock, dusted for fingerprints, while Sergeant Vanderleun, assisted by Pyke, set up his camera and began photographing the body, the desk, and the rest of the study from every angle. Dr. Melmoth began his examination of the corpse.

Meanwhile, Mallow and Sergeant Bellman retired to the hall with Higgins so the latter could deliver his report.

"Sit down, Higgins," said Mallow. "You've been on your feet a long time. And have some coffee," he added.

"Thank you, sir, I won't say no," said Higgins, accepting the proffered flask. Refreshed, he began his report. Mallow allowed him to give it uninterrupted; he had always maintained, since achieving rank, that knowing as much as possible before asking questions enabled him to ask better ones.

"Let me see if I have this clear," said Mallow when Higgins was done. "Mr. Oldfield was alive at seven o'clock, when the footman brought him his dinner. The butler found him dead shortly after ten o'clock. Between those times he preferred to be — no, insisted upon — being left alone. All right so far?"

"Yes, sir, that is correct."

"We'll see if we can corroborate those times. You found nothing out of the ordinary about the study?"

"Apart from the murder itself — the body, the bloodstained paperweight, and the disarranged dinner — no, sir. I do not know how the study usually appeared, though."

"Of course," said Mallow. "Neither do I. Perhaps the butler can help us there — or this Edwina Hackett. Who is she?"

"She did not say, beyond giving me her name and address."

"A singular sort of woman, though, to take such a cool attitude towards murder."

"I thought so myself, sir."

"Very well, Higgins — I think that will be all for now," said Mallow, standing up. "Time you went home and got some sleep. Do you need a lift?"

"Thank you, sir, but if you don't mind I'd rather stay and observe. I'd like to move into the plainclothes branch someday."

"Certainly you may stay," said Mallow, smiling. "Come, let's see how the rest of the crew is doing."

"Well, Bellman," said Mallow as they went back to the study, "I hope this doesn't turn into one of those locked-room affairs our mystery writers like so much."

"It's early in the case yet, sir," said Bellman.

"True. This Hackett person intrigues me. 'Wanted to see a murder investigation up close' indeed! Poking about the murder scene! If she disturbed anything, she'll see *some* aspects of police procedure up closer than she'll like."

Sergeant Vanderleun had finished photographing the body and the study and was now taking close-ups of the fingerprints which Sergeant Henley had found. Mallow was not surprised to hear from Henley that no prints had been found on the dragon paperweight.

Dr. Melmoth had finished his examination of the body and called in the stretcher-bearers. "Wait," said Mallow. "We need to see what's in his pockets."

They found only a handkerchief, a bunch of keys, a small sketching block and a drawing-pencil. No money, no letters, no pocket-book. Mallow nodded and the body was carried out to the van.

The removal of the body had revealed another sketching block on the desk. On the top sheet in straggling letters were a few words. Mallow leaned over to read them: *justis lik tortis.*

"Henley, you had better print this," said Mallow, "and Vanderleun, get a photograph."

No fingerprints were found on the paper, only smudges. After verifying the pencil on the floor had been printed and photographed, Mallow carefully removed the message and scribbled experimentally on the next sheet. Clearly this pencil, or one like it, had been used. He took out his notebook and copied the message, then handed the original to Henley to be taken back to headquarters for further study.

"A message pointing to the murderer?" commented Mallow. "Or random words written by a dazed and confused man?" He sounded them out. "Justice like tortoise? Well, it is, sometimes, but I can't say this gets us much farther."

"Excuse me," said Dr. Melmoth impatiently, "but do you want a preliminary report now or are you going to keep me waiting? We have to get the body back to Fenchester for the post-mortem, and I need my sleep."

"Sorry, Doctor," said Mallow. "Please say what you can now and then you can go."

"Not much to say. His head was bashed in." Dr. Melmoth confined his use of medical terminology to his written reports. "Probably by that paperweight. Could he have lived long enough to write that note? Could be, can't say — head injuries are funny. Time of death? Based on the body temperature — what time is it?"

"About two-thirty."

"Say four to five hours ago. Rigor's come on unusually fast, but rigor's a chancy thing. Tell you more after the post-mortem." Dr. Melmoth followed the men bearing the corpse out of the study and down the passage.

"Four to five hours," said Mallow. "That puts the murder between nine-thirty and ten-thirty last night; but he was dead at ten. Let's start poking about. I'll take the desk. Porlock and Pyke can go through the books on the shelves. Bellman, you take everything else. Higgins — you assist Sergeant Bellman."

"Yes, sir."

"Henley and Vanderleun can stand by in case we need anything more printed or photographed."

Mallow sat down at the desk, put on his spectacles, and began going through the drawers. Most were unlocked and, like Oldfield's pockets, devoid of anything of immediate significance. The entire contents comprised three more sketching blocks, two more drawing-pencils, several bars of chocolate, three packs of playing cards, and a quantity of caricatures. Mallow recognised one as William the footman; others were also of servants. Three were of a tall, thin, severe-looking man in a laboratory coat. One depicted with deadly precision a handsome but dissolute young man.

One of the drawers was locked. Mallow tried the keys on the bunch taken from Oldfield's pocket and found one that unlocked it. This drawer contained a cheque-book, a bottle of ink and a pen, and three sheets of writing paper. On one was written, line after line, the name "Sebastian Oldfield"; the writing starting out shakily but becoming firmer and neater on each succeeding line. Another was much the same, but the handwriting was different and the name was "Barnabas Merryweather." On the third, the writer was attempting the words "One thousand pounds" and the amount in figures, "£1,000." Mallow showed them to Henley. "Someone has been practising," he said. "Evidence of forgery? You're the handwriting expert — you had better take charge of these and the note... What kind of a name is Barnabas Merryweather? Are we in Conan Doyle or Charles Dickens?"

Bellman started with the French window. As had Edwina before him, he tried it and found it locked. Even unlocked, it could not have been opened: snow had drifted up against it twelve to fifteen inches deep and more snow had slid down from the roof. As far as he could see in the light from the study there were no footprints outside. He borrowed Oldfield's keys from Mallow, unlocked the window, and tried again. As he expected, it opened only a fraction of an inch before the piled-up snow stopped it.

He moved on to the armchair. Nothing under the chair, nothing under the seat cushion. There were a few scraps of paper on the floor. "Bad mark for the housemaid," he muttered.

"What?" asked Mallow.

"Nothing." Next came the book and the magazines on the table. He saw the rings on the book, held it up, and announced "Deplorable!"

"Eh?" said Mallow busy at the desk.

"*Look* at this. Someone's been putting his drinks down on Volume One of a *first edition* of *Sense and Sensibility*."

"Really? I agree — appalling. Perhaps Oldfield was killed by a bibliophile."

"Justifiable homicide, then," grumbled Bellman. *"Was ever Scythia half so barbarous?"* Mallow gave him a puzzled look. *"Titus Andronicus,* sir."

Higgins, remembering the toy trains of his childhood, elected to examine the model railway. Thoroughly to examine the whole of it would take at least an hour; but even with a few minutes' scrutiny he saw that Oldfield had been adept enough to run three trains simultaneously. Wishing to be thorough, he crawled under the table, bumped his head, and swore. He stuck his head out and said "Sorry." Mallow and Bellman noticed neither the oath nor the apology. Vanderleun looked disapproving; Henley gave him a friendly smile.

Higgins pulled his head back in and resumed his search. Finding nothing of significance — not even dust in the carpet — he came out, bumping his head again.

At the bookcases, Pyke and Porlock found a bewildering variety of works, covering everything from abnormal psychology to zymology. Mr. Oldfield, clearly, had been a scientific and technical polymath.

"Rhinoplasty," commented Porlock. "What the hell is that?"

"The science of plastic rhinoceroses, obviously," returned Pyke, deadpan.

"Save the crosstalk for another time, gentlemen," said Mallow. Having finished with the drawers of the desk, he was intrigued by the row of buttons. Less cautious than Edwina, he pushed the first one.

The door to the passage slid shut.

Interesting. He pushed the button again. The door slid open. *Makes sense — why get up and cross the room to open or close your door when you can do it from your desk?*

He tried another button. Up from the desk rose a small panel into which two dials were set, similar to those in the apparatus in the hall. Beneath each was a knob similar to the tuner on a wireless set. One was a clock; the other a temperature gauge with a range from -20° to 120°. *Ready for* all *kinds of weather.* Mallow lived in a country where a day in the eighties brought forth headlines; he tried to imagine a hundred and twenty degrees but gave up. He was about to try a third button when Bellman spoke.

"Sir? You may want to see this." The sergeant had opened the door in the alcove. Mallow walked over and looked through the doorway into a small space about six feet by ten. To the left were a Hoover and a shelf holding rags and bottles of cleanser and furniture polish. To the right a spiral staircase ran upwards.

"Aha!" he exclaimed. "So it's not a locked-room mystery after all."

Bellman objected. "Except the door *was* locked —" He held up Oldfield's set of keys. "— and the key is here."

"There could have been another key."

"Yes, sir — but look at these boxes that were piled up against it. The murderer might have come *in* this way, but not *out.* He couldn't have replaced the boxes."

"Good catch, Bellman," said Mallow. "I need more coffee. My brain's not at its best this time of day. Where does the staircase go?"

Bellman went up and came down again. "One flight up. There's a door at the top but it's locked. The key fits it."

Mallow was about to go back to the desk when Pyke and Higgins simultaneously spoke up. "Sir?"

"What is it, Pyke?"

"There's something very odd about the books on this shelf. On the other shelves they were tightly wedged, but move one and the rest were loose. Here — I can't move them at all."

Mallow came over and tried himself. Pyke was correct: the books could not be moved. The matched sizes, lettering on the spines, and the binding showed they formed a set that took up the entire shelf. Mallow looked at the titles: *The Uses of Phlogiston; A Case for Geocentricity; Humours, and How to Balance Them; Theory and Practice of Phrenology; Therapeutic Bloodletting; The Life and Times of Prester John; Shakespeare's Guide to Bacon...* Bellman, looking over Mallow's shoulder, suddenly snorted with laughter. "Dummies," he said. "Those aren't real titles." Mallow and Pyke tapped and prodded but could not determine their true nature.

"Now, Higgins — what have you found?" asked Mallow, giving up on the dummy books.

Higgins had been looking behind the prints in the alcove. "Here, sir." Handling it carefully by the edges, the constable took down a print that took pride of place among the others. It was one of those portraying a melodrama: a stern, upright gentleman with ginger hair and whiskers, bespectacled and clad in an indigo coat and tartan waistcoat, brandished a roll of paper. A young woman in white knelt before him, pleading; seated in the background was an elderly man, dejected, his head in his hands. The title of the print was "The Virtuous Villain."

Mallow looked at the print. "Foreclosing on the mortgage, no doubt," he commented. "What does it have to do with the murder?

"No, sir — on the wall." Higgins pointed.

"I don't see — oh, yes, I do." A rectangular piece of the panel, two inches by three, was outlined by an almost imperceptible gap. He raised his hand to it.

"Fingerprints, sir," warned Henley.

"Good God, my brain *is* tired," said Mallow. "Go to it."

Henley dusted the rectangle. There were no prints. Mallow pressed it gently and felt it give. He pressed harder. It swung out, revealing yet another button.

"Good work, Higgins," said Mallow. He yawned. A moment later, so did everyone else in the study. "It's what, nearly four? Henley, print the button and the inside knob of the staircase door — and the door at the top while you're at it. Vanderleun, once you've photographed the prints, you and Henley take one of the cars and return to headquarters. Get your photos of the prints developed as soon as possible so that we can send them up to London and show them to the Yard. Take Higgins with you and drop him off in Minstrel Folly."

"Thank you, sir," said Higgins. "

"I'll leave it to the butler to explain what this button does."

When the constable and the sergeants had departed, Mallow, Bellman, Pyke, and Porlock made an inch-by-inch examination of the floor. *So that's what you meant by that remark about the housemaid,* thought Mallow, discovering for himself the scraps of paper.

By half-past four the search was over. Mallow and the rest returned to the hall. Bellman, Porlock, and Pyke soon fell asleep. Mallow dozed, waking up from time to time only to see how little time had passed.

3

POLICE INVESTIGATION IS NOT A SPECTATOR SPORT

At seven o'clock a housemaid came into the hall, saw Mallow and the others, squeaked "Oooh!" and retreated. Mallow awoke Bellman and the constables and they waited patiently. Eventually Pembert entered — Mallow recognised him at once from Oldfield's caricature. "You must be the police," said the butler. "William left a note you had arrived."

After introducing himself and his colleagues, Mallow said, "I take it you are Pembert — the butler?"

"Yes, sir." Mallow was struck by Pembert's deference. In his experience, butlers considered themselves socially a cut above policemen, even officers.

"Who is in authority here now? I should like to speak with them before anyone else."

Pembert did not reply immediately. Finally he said, "I suppose I am, sir. Mr. Cabell left yesterday evening on a journey to Town and did not plan to return until tomorrow. However, I have rung him up at his hotel and informed him of the — the occurrence. Mr. Cabell said he will hire a car and arrive as soon as he can today."

"And Mr. Cabell is?"

"He is Mr. Oldfield's laboratory assistant, and also acts as his secretary."

"Mr. Oldfield has no family living here?"

"No, sir. Mr. Oldfield's only relative is his nephew, Charles Muirdyke. Mr. Muirdyke visits from time to time, but resides in London. I have attempted to reach him at his flat but it appears he is not there."

Mallow turned to Constable Pyke. "Now's your chance to practise your shorthand, Pyke." The constable took out a notebook to record the interview. "Now, I understand it was you that found Mr. Oldfield."

"Yes, sir."

"Please give me the details."

Pembert repeated what he had told Constable Higgins.

"You said you went to him?"

"Yes. I put my hand on his neck, to see if there was a pulse — I have a little First Aid experience. He felt warm — almost feverish — so I thought at first he had been suddenly taken ill. But there was no pulse, and then I saw his head —" Pembert stopped.

"The body was warm?"

"Yes, sir."

"Did you see anyone, or hear anyone moving about, as you were bringing the whisky?"

"No."

"Can you explain the purpose of that unusual door?"

"The door was one of Mr. Oldfield's inventions. Mr. Oldfield disliked anyone coming into a room he was in without warning. The door cannot be opened from the outside without the key, so anyone wishing to enter must knock; he would then open the door, and close it when his visitor left. I and the other staff at first took it hard that we were not trusted properly to close a door, but soon it just became one of Mr. Oldfield's ways."

"How many people besides you and Mr. Oldfield had keys?"

"Only Mr. Cabell."

"What can you tell me about Mr. Oldfield?"

"He was a good master. He had his little ways, as I said." Pembert hesitated.

"Go on. Don't worry about protecting his reputation. Anything you tell me can't hurt him, and if it's irrelevant it won't come out."

"Oh, no, sir," said Pembert, shocked. "Nothing like that."

"Merely eccentric, then?"

"Some might say so. Mr. Oldfield was a very private man. As far as I know, he had no friends, no associates save Mr. Cabell, and no visitors except on business."

"What about Miss Hackett?"

"Miss Hackett is here in a professional capacity. She is painting Mr. Oldfield's portrait."

"Do you know if Mr. Oldfield had any enemies?"

"No, sir. Mr. Oldfield was always a pleasant, considerate, even-tempered man."

"I see. What else can you tell me?"

"Mr. Oldfield was regular in his habits. He always had breakfast in bed, then rose, bathed, dressed — himself, he did not have a valet — and descended to the study. He cleaned the study —"

"Also himself?" asked Mallow. *Eccentric, indeed.*

"Yes," replied Pembert. "The study was his room and his alone. He was very particular about keeping it clean — very tidy in everything. Later in the day he usually went to confer with Mr. Cabell in the workshop behind the manor house for an hour or so. Afterwards, if the weather was good he spent time in the garden with his roses; otherwise he went back to the study. Mid-afternoon he retired to his bedroom for a nap. He did not take tea. At seven o'clock he dined."

"In the study?"

"Yes. As I told the constable, he almost always dined there, unless entertaining a guest on business. He would remain there, alone, until I brought him his whisky-and-soda at ten — although if Mr. Charles was visiting, he was invited to spend time with his uncle there after his dinner."

"Was it usual for William to bring Mr. Oldfield's dinner?"

"Yes. Sometimes I did."

"Has there been any change in his behaviour recently? Any sign he was worried?"

Pembert did not reply at first. Finally, he said, "Last September, quite suddenly, he began to have occasional migraine headaches. Mr. Cabell urged him to see a physician but he refused, saying he knew how to deal with them."

"How did he deal with them?"

"Usually he lay down in his bedroom with the blinds down and the lights off, except for one small reading lamp. Then he had me read to him, or Mr. Muirdyke if he was visiting."

"Anything else?"

"Occasionally he said he needed a change of scenery and asked me to drive him into Chiltonbury."

"For any particular reason?"

"I don't really know. He always told me to drop him off in the Market Square. I would then go to the cinema. Afterwards I would pick him up again in the square. I suppose he just walked about.

"I should add that, starting about mid-November the migraines became more frequent. At first — that is, starting in September — he had perhaps one a week; lately he had been having two or even three. Again Mr. Cabell asked him to seek treatment but he would not. When Mr. Oldfield had made up his mind there was no moving him, no matter how hard one pushed."

"Are you getting all this, Pyke?" asked Mallow.

"Yes, sir," replied the constable.

"Now, Pembert," said Mallow, "You said only Mr. Oldfield, yourself, and Mr. —"

"Cabell."

"— Mr. Cabell had keys to the door from the passage into the study. What about the French window?"

"Only Mr. Oldfield had the key to that one. He and I had the key to the ones in the library."

"And the door to the staircase?"

"Only Mr. Oldfield."

"Where does the stair go?"

"Up to Mr. Oldfield's bedroom, which is directly over the study."

"One last question. When you were in the study last night, did you see anything out of the ordinary? Apart from the murder itself, of course."

Pembert considered for several moments and then said, "No, sir, I did not."

"Thank you, Pembert, I think that will be all. No — I almost forgot. There is a button in the wall of the study, behind one of the prints. What does it do?"

A faint smile crossed the butler's face. "It opens a concealed door into the library."

Mallow and Bellman exchanged glances. *Another* way in and out?

"Also one of Mr. Oldfield's eccentricities?" asked the inspector.

"Yes, sir."

"Please show it to me."

Mallow and his colleagues accompanied the butler to the study. Pembert pressed the button and the panel shifted slightly. "This will have to be printed," remarked Mallow as he wrapped a handkerchief around his hand. He pushed and the panel swung back. From beyond came a thud and muffled clatter. Mallow let go and the panel closed again.

"Oh, dear," gasped Pembert. "I had forgot Miss Hackett's painting things." He rushed out of the study.

"Wait here," said Mallow. He followed Pembert into the library.

"— sorry, Miss Hackett," Pembert was saying to a sleepy-eyed young woman who was struggling to uncurl herself in an armchair. "I thought you had gone to — that is, I thought you had retired."

The young woman got up, yawned and stretched and ran a hand over her tousled blonde hair. "I must have fallen asleep. Did I miss the police?" Her gaze shifted past Pembert to Mallow. "Oh! Hullo, you are —?"

"Detective-Inspector Mallow. I take it you are Edwina Hackett?"

"That's me. I'm so glad to meet you." She came forward briskly and held out her hand. Involuntarily Mallow took it. "Have you found out who did it?"

"We're still investigating."

"Oh, good. What was that racket?"

"I fear we have disarranged your studio, Miss Hackett," said Pembert.

Edwina jumped up. A portion of the library had been screened off. She hurried behind the screen. "Oh, *Lord!*" She came out again and glared at Mallow. "Are you responsible for this?"

"I'm afraid so."

Edwina cast her eyes to the ceiling. "And I thought 'blundering bobbies' was a cliché of the thrillers," she said. "Just what sort of clues were you looking for in there?"

"It was my fault," interposed Pembert. "I was showing the inspector the concealed door in the study —"

"A secret door?" cried Edwina. Her anger evaporated, curiosity taking its place. "Oh, I must see!" She darted past Mallow out of the library and into the study. Encountering Bellman, she stopped and said "Another one?"

The sergeant, at a loss, did not answer.

"Where's the door? It must be in that wall." Edwina crossed the study. She noticed the button at once and pressed it. "Wonderful!" she exclaimed as the panel moved. Before Mallow could stop her Edwina had opened the door and gone through.

The inspector sighed. "It's going to be a job keeping up with that young woman... I don't know if it opens from the other side, or if she knows how. If she comes back, make her wait."

He found Edwina in what Pembert had called her studio. When the door had first been opened, a section of the bookshelves had swung out, upsetting an easel and a small table. Edwina had set the latter upright and was picking up brushes and tubes of paint scattered over the cloth laid down to protect the carpet.

"You're an artist, then, Miss Hackett?" asked Mallow, putting the easel on its legs.

"Portrait painter, mostly," replied Edwina. "That's why I'm here. I'd been commissioned to paint Mr. Oldfield." A thought struck her. "He won't be sitting for his portrait any more. I'll have to finish it from memory."

Mallow set the unfinished portrait on the easel and donned his spectacles to examine it more closely. Oldfield had not looked his best in the study and this was the inspector's first chance to get a clear look at the man. The portrait showed a stout man of about fifty. Only the head and face of the inventor were detailed. Enough had been sketched in below to show he was seated, with a closed book on his lap. One hand rested on the book; the other lay on the arm of his chair. His face, while not handsome, was not unpleasant. Grey eyes looked out from beneath arched, bushy brows. Below were an aquiline nose, a wide mouth, and a square, solid chin. Above was a full head of dark-red hair shot with grey.

The pose was a three-quarter view, so the sitter did not look directly at the viewer. The grey eyes were focused on a point far distant; together with the slight drawing together of the brows they suggested the mind behind them was busily at work on some problem. The mouth, relaxed and slightly curved, hinted the problem was solved, or nearly so. Of course, Mallow reflected, an inventor's mind would always be occupied with solving problems.

Edwina finished tidying up. Mallow, who had never known any artists, but had the impression they were Bohemian and careless, was surprised to see her gear laid out with the precision of an operating theatre.

The remainder of the studio's furnishings comprised the sitter's chair with its back to the opening and a lamp positioned to illuminate the sitter's face from above and to one side.

"I must ask you some questions, Miss Hackett," said Mallow.

"Of course," replied Edwina. "Please, just give me a minute." She left the library. In the passage she encountered Pembert.

"As it appears the police will be staying here some time yet," said the butler, "I have taken it upon myself to see that a breakfast has been placed in the hall."

"Thank you. Please tell the Inspector and his men. They're in the library and the study."

Edwina returned to the hall, where Pembert had laid out coffee and tea, cups, cream and sugar, and a tray of sandwiches. Mallow and his colleagues were there, but had not started eating. "Oh!" she said. "You needn't have waited for me. You must all be famished." She at once sat down and assumed the role of hostess, pouring out for the others and handing round the sandwiches.

In the library and the study, Mallow had not had a chance to get a clear picture of Edwina. Now, he seized the opportunity.

Sitting opposite him was a young woman of perhaps twenty-three or -four. Although she had tidied her hair, Edwina's creased grey jumper and dark-blue skirt testified to her night in the library chair. Her features were unremarkable; her mouth a little too broad and her teeth, though white, decidedly irregular; but offsetting these defects were her large hazel eyes, no longer sleepy, but filled with and alert intelligence.

Edwina, for her part, studied Mallow with the eyes of a portrait painter. Hair, black; parted on the right. Eyes, bright blue, under level black brows. Nose, a trifle long, but straight. Mouth, good. Chin, firm. Overall, angular: good bones. He wasn't what she expected of a country policeman. The sergeant beside him looked more the part, being square and fiftyish, with mild brown eyes and a grizzled moustache. The Inspector was clean-shaven and could not have been much past thirty.

"If it's proper to ask questions during a meal, go right ahead," she said.

"Very well," said Mallow.

Constable Pyke took out his notebook and opened it to a fresh page.

"You said you were here to paint Mr. Oldfield's portrait?" began Mallow.

"Yes. The *Panopticon* is doing a series of articles about Notable British Inventors and they wanted a picture of him. They asked for a photograph, but Mr. Oldfield refused to allow a photographer to come to the manor, and refused to go to them, so they compromised on me."

"And how long have you been here?"

"I came here a week ago. I spent the first day setting everything up, then got to work. I hadn't got very far. Mr. Oldfield could never sit for long — usually an hour at a time, sometimes a little more, sometimes a little less. Mr. Cabell would always come in and haul him off to the workshop."

"Please tell me what you can about last night," said Mallow.

"It was a good sitting. Mr. Cabell came in briefly to say he was leaving for London at seven and had to pack, so Mr. Oldfield was able to sit for over an hour, from 5:00 to about 6:30. Then he went to his study. I stayed in the studio working on the background of the painting and then sat down with a book. That was it, until Pembert came in a little after ten with the news of the murder."

"And then?"

"Pembert called the police station and reported the murder. Then he went back to the study. He stayed outside while I went in and looked about — I've read a lot of stories about murders but never seen one, and my curiosity got the better of me." Edwina gave Mallow a wide-eyed stare and a little smile.

"Constable Higgins informed me of that. It was very wrong of you to enter the study," Mallow rebuked her. "You might have seriously impeded the investigation and caused a great deal of trouble not only for us but also for yourself."

"I didn't touch *anything*," Edwina protested. "No — I'm wrong — I tried the French window. Oh, and the other door. But I used a handkerchief so I wouldn't disturb any fingerprints. Still, you're right — next murder I'll behave better."

"Sebastian Oldfield was not murdered for your amusement, Miss Hackett!" said Mallow with genuine severity.

"I deserved that," said Edwina after a short pause. "I'm always putting my foot in it. Dad was forever telling me my mouth moved twice as fast as my brain. I *am* sorry. Please carry on — I'll be good."

"I shall overlook it — this time," said Mallow. "Constable Higgins informed me you were in the library the entire evening. When did you leave the studio?"

"Just before seven. I saw William pass by with Mr. Oldfield's dinner."

"And you saw no one until Pembert at ten?"

"Yes."

"Might you have been absorbed in your book?"

"*War and Peace* is *not* an absorbing book. I've been trying to read it for years — I always get stuck somewhere, and then I get interrupted and forget the plot and have to go back and start over."

"Are you sure, then, you didn't fall asleep?"

"I *told* the constable — I never doze. When I'm not wide awake I'm fast asleep, and contrariwise."

Bellman and Porlock had finished eating while Mallow was speaking with Edwina. He directed them to go talk to the staff and find out which, if any, had alibis. Then he resumed his questioning.

"Did you hear anything when William was in the study?"

"Nothing clearly until just before he came out. I heard Mr. Oldfield call out, 'Thank you, William,' then the door closed — you can't mistake the noise it makes, a sort of hiss — and William passed the library door on his way back down the passage."

"And when Pembert was in the study at ten?"

"I didn't hear anything."

"You might not have, if the study door was closed."

"But it wasn't. As I just said, you can hear it close. Besides, when I went back with Pembert, it was still open."

"Did Mr. Oldfield converse with you during the sittings?"

"No," answered Edwina, "nor I with him. Sometimes my sitters talk, sometimes they don't. I like it when they do — it animates their faces and gives me insight into their characters — but I don't insist upon it. Anyway, this time insisting would have had no effect — Mr. Cabell told me when he engaged me that Mr. Oldfield was extremely shy and any conversation would make him very uncomfortable. Fortunately, he was a strong personality and projected well; in his case I didn't really need him to talk."

"Thank you, Miss Hackett," said Mallow. "I don't think I need bother you with any more questions. However, I must ask that, for the time being, you remain here at Minstrel Manor."

William entered the hall to clear away the remains of breakfast. "Ah — William," said Mallow. "Please stay a moment."

Edwina showed no signs of leaving, but sat, alert and interested, sipping her coffee. Mallow looked meaningfully at her, but Edwina ignored the hint. "Miss Hackett," he finally said, "will you please leave?"

"Why?" asked Edwina.

"I must talk to William."

"Talk away. I'll just sit here quiet as a mouse. I want to watch you do your stuff."

"Miss Hackett," said Mallow, exasperated, "police investigation is *not* a spectator sport!"

"Oh, very well." Setting down her coffee, Edwina stood up and walked back toward the library. But as she did so, she picked up one of the gilt chairs and carried it with her out of the hall. Mallow watched her: as soon as she turned the corner of the passage, she set down the chair and sat in it, well within earshot.

Short of arresting her at once, Mallow decided, there was nothing he could do; so he merely invited William to sit down. At first the footman refused, but Mallow repeated the invitation and William, pale and nervous, sat down on the very edge of one of the armchairs.

"Now, William, I have only a few questions for you," said Mallow kindly. "I understand you brought Mr. Oldfield's dinner to him last night as usual?"

William gulped, hesitated, and finally brought out, "Yes, sir."

"Please tell me what happened."

"Well, sir, I brought it along at seven sharp, like I always do," said William, gaining confidence. "Mr. Oldfield, 'e was keen on things being done on time. If you were even a little late, 'e'd let you know."

"How? Was he angry?"

"Oh, no, sir. 'E'd only always say something like, 'Bungled the business, William', or 'Missed your cue, William'."

"I see. On this particular occasion, however, you were punctual?"

"Yes, sir. Dinner at seven sharp, like I said."

"Did Mr. Oldfield seem upset, or uneasy, or in any way different from his usual self?"

William did not answer immediately. Finally he said, "Not exactly, sir. Not upset. If anything, 'e seemed cheerful, sort of 'appy-like, like 'e'd 'ad good news."

"Did he say anything to give you this impression?"

"No, sir, 'e just said 'Thank you, William'. It was the *way* 'e said it."

"How did Mr. Oldfield seem to you usually?"

"'E was pretty much always the same, pleasant-like, but not chatty. I'd bring 'im 'is breakfast and 'e'd say thanks and then 'Fine day, William, isn't it?' or something like that. 'E always treated you like a 'uman being, not like Mr. Cabell —" William realised he was crossing a line and stopped.

"Yes, William, how did Mr. Cabell treat you?" prompted Mallow.

"Well, sir — Mr. Cabell, 'e acts like you're not there. You take 'im 'is lunch in the workshop and 'e doesn't say anything, doesn't even look at you. Or if 'e's going from one room to another and you're in 'is way, 'e walks around you like you were a piece of furniture. Or if Mr.

Oldfield was there, Mr. Cabell would be nattering away about some invention or other, going sixteen to the dozen, and Mr. Oldfield yawning like 'e'd 'eard it all before. I said to Sallie — she's one of the 'ousemaids — I said to 'er the other day, Sallie, if a two-'eaded 'ippopotamus brought Mr. Cabell 'is lunch, 'e'd never notice it."

Mallow had no further questions for William, so the interview ended on this flight of fancy.

As William left, Bellman and Porlock returned. "Well, sir," said Bellman, "if any one of the staff is in it, they're all in it. They all alibi each other for the entire period from just after seven, when William returned from bringing Oldfield his dinner, to just before ten, when Pembert went out with the whisky."

"I was afraid that would be the case, Bellman," said Mallow. "Miss Hackett has complicated the case. She told me the same story she told Higgins: she was in the library from seven to ten, sitting where she could see into the passage, and no one went to or from the study the entire time."

"Can we rely on Miss Hackett's word, sir?"

"I don't know." He raised his voice slightly. "She seems to be something of a flibbertigibbet —" He lowered it again. "— But honest. Still, we must definitely take a close look at her."

The discussion was interrupted by the roaring of a powerful engine from outside. It stopped and was followed by the opening of the front door and the entry of a young man in tweeds, fair-haired and clean-shaven save for a wispy moustache. He stopped short when he saw the policemen, then came forward and said, "I say, what's up?"

4

HE WAS HAULING ME OVER THE COALS

Once more Mallow introduced himself and the others. "I am here investigating —"

"Good Lord!" exclaimed the young man. "A real live Detective-Inspector in the house! What is it — the kitchenmaid pinching the spoons, or a sinister foreigner snooping in Uncle Sebastian's workshop?"

Mallow mentally cursed the stars which had inflicted not one but two frivolous young people upon him. "Uncle Sebastian?" he said. "Then you would be Mr. Charles Muirdyke?"

"The same," said the young man. Looking at him, Mallow realised here was another subject of Oldfield's caricatures, although in person appearing slightly less dissipated.

"I'm afraid it is more serious than that, Mr. Muirdyke," said Mallow. "Your uncle was killed last night."

"Killed?" cried Muirdyke. "Was it an accident, or —"

"There's little doubt it was murder," said Mallow.

"Good Lord!" exclaimed Muirdyke again, and collapsed into a chair. "Who killed him?"

"That is what we are trying to find out, sir."

"How — how did it happen?"

"Mr. Oldfield was killed in his study. It appears he was struck on the head with the paperweight which was on his desk."

Muirdyke did not respond to this. He stared into space, muttering "Good Lord," over and over. On a table beside his chair was the hall telephone. He picked up the receiver and pushed a button. "A large brandy to the hall, at once… What? This is Mr. Charles speaking."

Presently Pembert entered bearing a snifter of brandy. Muirdyke seized it and downed half its contents. "Thank you, Pembert — that helped," he said.

"It is good to see you again, Mr. Charles," replied Pembert, "although I wish the circumstances were less melancholy."

Pembert departed. Muirdyke drank the rest of the brandy and said, "Where do we go from here?"

"You have just arrived from London?" asked Mallow.

"Got here last night, actually," said Muirdyke. "I was delayed — beastly weather! — and didn't reach the village until eight. I stopped at the Green Wyvern — that's the village pub — for supper and realised I was dead tired and didn't feel like ploughing up to the manor through the snow, so I got a room. Went up for a wash and brush-up and lay down with a book — Roland Cole's latest, *Horror in Hertfordshire,* dashed good thriller — and fell asleep. Woke up a couple of hours later and went downstairs. The pub was closed by then so Joe — he's the landlord — and I had a game or two of darts and I went to bed again. Slept straight through to this morning and came up here."

Here was another suspect. Mallow made a mental note that Muirdyke's movements would have to be checked.

"How well did you know your uncle?" he asked.

"Not very well, but probably better than anyone except, maybe, John Cabell. If you've talked to him you'll know Uncle Sebastian kept himself pretty much *to* himself — no friends, not even any acquaintances. He made an exception for me — I was the only family he had. My mother — she died ten years ago — was his sister. After his inventing business took off he took care of us — paid for my schooling, that sort of thing. Once I was out of school he made me an allowance of £200 a year."

"Would you have known if he had any enemies?"

"If he did, he never mentioned it. But he never talked about himself or his work."

"What did he talk about?"

"Mostly his hobbies: roses, model railways, and the theatre — especially the theatre. Quite often I was the audience while he recited Shakespeare, or one of those blood-and-thunder melodramas he was so fond of. No, that's not quite right — he didn't recite a play, he *acted* it. He must have had dozens of plays memorised, for he could do any one of them start to finish, and hit off all the characters dashed well. It's a shame he was such a recluse — he could have gone in for amateur theatricals in a really big way."

"Anything else?"

"No. The rest of the time he was hauling me over the coals for something or other."

"Were you and he on bad terms then?"

"Good Lord, no! Uncle Sebastian was *concerned* about me. He was always after me to make something of myself — why couldn't I keep a job, cut back on drinking, stop playing the ponies, that sort of thing. He kept saying he didn't want me to find out what it was like to be a drunkard and a failure, not able to earn an honest shilling — I was still young enough to change my ways. Then he'd tell Cabell to give me a cheque for fifty or a hundred pounds, and say he hoped I wouldn't spend it foolishly." Muirdyke's face fell. "Poor Uncle Sebastian! I was going to tell him I had got another job — I've been taken on as an assistant buyer by Todd and Hallam — big wines-and-spirits firm in London. I start next week."

"One more question, Mr. Muirdyke — can you tell me the name of Mr. Oldfield's solicitor?"

"Sorry, no. You'll have to ask Cabell... Would this be about Uncle Sebastian's will?"

"Among other things."

"Well, unless he changed his mind recently, he's left something to each of the staff, a little extra to Pembert, a fairish bit to Cabell and the rest to me, since I'm his only relative. He always spoke of it quite openly." Muirdyke sighed and went on, "Dash it all, now I *will* have to be responsible — it won't do to let the old boy down."

"I suppose not," said Mallow. "Thank you, Mr. Muirdyke. Oh — one more thing. We are going to have to search the premises. I apologise for the intrusion — it's a matter of routine, you see. I have a warrant with me if you wish to see it."

"Oh, good Lord, *I* don't mind," said Muirdyke. "Cabell is a bit touchy about the workshop — you may want to wait until he's here before looking at it. Nobody but he and Uncle Sebastian had a key to it anyway... I'd better go talk to the staff and let them know what's coming."

"I've already spoken to them, sir," said Bellman. "There will be no problem there."

"I'll go talk to them anyway," said Muirdyke. "Let them know I'm here and all that — good Lord, I suppose they'll have to look to me now if they have problems or need instructions. How dashed feudal." With this remark Muirdyke left the hall.

"Bellman," said Mallow, "take Porlock and search the servants' quarters; and, while you're there, get the fingerprints of each member of the staff — you're sure there won't be a problem?"

"Quite sure, sir. One or two of the younger girls may come over queer, but they'll do what Pembert or the housekeeper tell them."

"If there's a cellar, search that next. Pyke and I will go over the rest of the ground floor." Mallow added in a slightly louder voice, "*Starting with the library,*" and continued, "after that, we'll tackle the upper floors."

Mallow's warning brought Edwina out of her thoughts. She moved quickly into the library. When Mallow and Pyke arrived, they found her back in her chair with *War and Peace.* "Hullo again, Inspector," she said, smiling.

"Would you mind leaving, Miss Hackett?" asked Mallow.

"Oh, mayn't I stay?"

"I thought I said police investigation is not —"

"I shan't get in your way. Please?"

It had been a long night and looked like being a longer day. Mallow was on the point of exploding when he remembered Pyke. He went to a window, counted ten silently while gazing out at the snow, turned, and said, "Very well." He went into the passage, took the gilt chair, and set it in the library doorway. "Sit there. If you stir from that chair, Constable Pyke —" Pyke at once assumed an expression of grim determination. "— will escort you elsewhere."

Edwina obeyed.

The library and study together made up one of the new wings of the manor; the former, taking up two-thirds of the wing, was therefore longer than it was deep. The shelves that lined it were interrupted only by the door into the passage, two French windows on the opposite side, and a bay window at the end away from the study. Wooden chairs were placed at two long tables bearing green-shaded lamps, for the use of the serious researcher, while several comfortable wing chairs upholstered with fabric in muted colors invited the casual reader.

The books on the shelves were mostly of two kinds. The first was old books. Mallow opened one at random and found it had been printed in MDCXXXIII; it took his tired mind some moments to translate this to 1633. *Good thing Bellman isn't here — we'd have to use force to get him out.* These were mostly religious works: volumes of sermons, devotional books, theological treatises. The other comprised matched sets of expensively-bound classics, but they gave the impression of having been bought more for their value as décor than their value as literature. On one shelf a number of books, inscribed on their fly-leaves by Charles Muirdyke, showed the young man's taste ran to the more lurid and thrilling kind of detective fiction.

Having finished his examination of the shelves, Mallow went to the entrance to the screened-off studio, paused, and called out, "Miss Hackett? Would you please be so kind as to come and move your things? I need to look at the shelves here."

Edwina complied. Pyke assisted her by moving the easel. When she was done she placed herself just outside and watched as Mallow examined the books and then searched for a way to open the concealed door. Unsuccessful after several minutes, he called Pyke away from contemplating Oldfield's portrait and asked him to try.

Edwina went to the telephone and asked for Pembert. They exchanged a few words; she hung up and returned to the studio. "Inspector?" she said.

"What?"

"I can open it for you." She went at once to the shelves; Mallow politely stood aside. Edwina stooped and removed *Oliver Twist* from the bottom shelf. She put her hand in the space the book had occupied, groped about, and pushed. The door opened.

"How did you know to do that?" demanded Mallow. "And why didn't you tell us?"

"I asked Pembert, just now," replied Edwina.

"I see," said Mallow. *I should have thought of that myself.* After a moment he added, "Thank you."

"You're quite welcome. Are you finished here? I'd like to work on the painting."

"Yes." As Mallow left the studio he collided with Muirdyke.

"Dashed sorry," said Muirdyke. "Didn't see you coming. Came here for a book, saw the screen, and came over for a look-see. I say, what a neat set-out." He dropped into the sitter's chair, noticed Edwina, and stood up again. "Good morning."

"Good morning," she replied.

"I say, Inspector," said Muirdyke, "your Sergeant Bellman has quite a way with the servants. I thought at least they'd make a row about being fingerprinted, but they were meek as mice."

"I'm afraid we'll have to take your fingerprints also, Mr. Muirdyke," said Mallow. "And yours too, Miss Hackett."

"Good Lord," said Muirdyke. "Hackett? The brush-and-canvas lady?"

"Yes," said Edwina, amused. "I don't believe we've been introduced. Inspector, would you please oblige?"

Mallow was slightly disconcerted by Edwina's impish request. He had never expected that part of a Detective-Inspector's job was to introduce principals in a murder case to each other; nevertheless, with grave courtesy he performed this little ceremony.

"I'm dashed pleased to meet you, Miss Hackett," said Muirdyke. "I heard about you from Uncle Sebastian the last time I was here — he told me a young lady named Hackett was coming to paint his picture. He was quite looking forward to your visit."

"Was he?" replied Edwina. "I'm flattered."

Muirdyke sat down again. "Must be dashed interesting, having your portrait done. Nothing like photography, is it? How long would I have to sit — hours and hours, I suppose."

"Something like that," said Edwina.

"I say, how about a stroll down to the pub while the coppers are going through the house? It's a fine sunny morning — cold, but not too windy."

"Thank you, Mr. Muirdyke. I should enjoy that very much."

Edwina and Muirdyke delayed their departure so that Constable Pyke could take their fingerprints: a procedure in which both took a lively interest.

The search of the rest of the house drew a series of blanks. Sebastian Oldfield's bedroom yielded nothing more than another heap of illustrated magazines and some newspapers. John Cabell's bedroom yielded nothing at all; if he had any personal life, it was elsewhere.

Edwina Hackett traveled light — apart from her painting gear, which was in the studio, she had brought only a few changes of clothes.

"Now for the workshop," said Mallow. "Oh — before I forget. We must put seals on all the entries into the study. I wouldn't put it past that young woman to try her hand at amateur detection."

Behind the manor stood the workshop: a windowless and graceless concrete block utterly at odds with the simple Georgian elegance of the house.

"Do we wait for Cabell?" asked Pyke.

"Cabell will have to lump it," replied Mallow. By now he was longing for sleep. He tried Oldfield's keys until one fit and unlocked the door. Inside it was dark; Bellman found the switch and turned on the lights. In their harsh white glare the inside of the workshop looked even less inviting than the outside.

An uncarpeted passage ran almost the full length of one side of the workshop before turning to the left at the far end. Doors spaced at intervals along the inside wall of the passage opened into: a chemical laboratory; a metalworking and carpentry shop; a room lined with cages of small animals and a variety of plants in glass boxes; and another filled with intricate and enigmatic machines, most bearing small placards reading "Caution - Danger - Do Not Touch".

Beyond the turn in the passage were two offices, each furnished with a desk and several chairs, a draughting board and stool, and bookshelves and file cabinets. The similarity ended with the furniture. One office was neat and tidy: bound volumes of scientific and technical journals filled the shelves; a few folders lay squarely on the desk; and fastened to the draughting board was a half-completed drawing of an intricate and incomprehensible mechanism. The office was immaculately clean, without even a speck of dust anywhere.

The other office was a study in chaos. Books and papers were piled on every available surface, even the draughting board. Scattered among them were pencils, big and little metal wheels, tools, and bits of wood and wire. The walls were lined with corkboard to which were pinned innumerable little notes.

A door at the end of the short leg of the passage opened into a large storage room filled with jars and bottles of chemicals, shelves piled high with electrical and mechanical apparatus, and stacks of sheet metal, lumber, and rubber tubing. Here also were a softly humming generator and some drums of petrol.

The first office was quickly disposed of. Spaced at regular intervals on the walls were framed letters from manufacturers, industrialists, and hospitals and other institutions, all thanking Sebastian Oldfield for some invention which had improved the efficiency, or extended the scope, of their operations. Among them was a copy of an approved patent application for unbreakable glass.

The file cabinets, curiously, were empty. In the drawers of the desk Mallow found nothing of significance: some pens and pencils, a well-used pack of cards, two bars of chocolate, and a large bag of toffee. A store of caricatures concealed under the desk blotter indicated this office belonged to Mr. Oldfield. Several depicted the same tall, thin man as the one in the sketch found in the study; from the fact that he wore a laboratory coat in most of them, Mallow concluded the subject was John Cabell. The caricatures showed considerable talent and a touch of broad comedy: Cabell in a before-and-after sketch grasping a mouse and pouring something into its mouth from a beaker, then cowering back from the mouse, which was now eight feet tall and hugely fanged; Cabell tripping over a bucket and falling into a machine labeled "DANGER" as electrical sparks played about him; Cabell, not in his coat but clad as a stage magician, pulling a guinea pig from a hat. There was also a caricature of Oldfield himself, brandishing a bubbling test tube in one hand and a lightning bolt in the other while borne upon a vast shadowy figure.

"If I have seen further than others, it is because I have stood on the shoulders of giants," said Bellman.

"Eh?" said Mallow.

"Isaac Newton said that when praised for his genius," replied Bellman. "Oldfield seems to have agreed."

"And had rather a high opinion of himself."

Returning to the second office, Mallow looked about and wondered where to begin. Selecting at random a pile of papers, he began to go through it. Near the top was a thick notebook labeled "Experimental Results." There was a bookmark in it; he opened the book at the marked page to discover a grid of squares and rectangles labeled with the names of various grains and vegetables: wheat, barley, and rye; potatoes, carrots, and mangel-wurzels. Each contained a number, a chemical formula — incomprehensible to Mallow — and a green, yellow, or red dot. Most of the dots were red. "Here, Porlock," he said. "Take charge of this. Go through it and see if you can make anything of it." He opened a drawer in one of the file cabinets and found it full. "Bellman, you can look into these. Pyke and I will keep on with the papers."

5

THE GREEN WYVERN

Minstrel Manor faced northwest, away from the morning sun; nevertheless, stepping out of the front door of the house, Edwina and Muirdyke were dazzled. Everywhere was snow, piled into drifts or clinging in great clumps to the trees. Intermixed with it were myriads upon myriads of minute crystals of ice which caught the morning sun and reflected it sparkling in every direction. Wherever the sunlight did not fall was pure blue shadow. In the distance was Darkling Hill, the lone eminence of Fenshire, its ominous bulk shrouded in white. To the left of the hill and further off, the sun lit the cross atop Chiltonbury Cathedral.

"I say," said Muirdyke, looking about. "This is a bit of all right, what?"

"Oh, yes," replied Edwina. She took a deep breath. The frigid air stung her nose but refreshed her nonetheless. "Much better than being cooped up in — I can't say it's a *gloomy* house, but it's certainly not a *cheerful* one. Even an exciting murder — oh, I *am* sorry."

"Don't be," said Muirdyke. "I'll miss the old boy, of course — he was the only family I had, and he did his best for me — but more than anything else I'm surprised he got himself killed. Nobody knew him well enough to dislike him — as I said to the inspector, he kept himself *to* himself."

"Do you know why?"

"No. I've only known him for ten years or so. I knew *of* him before then, from my mother. He had run away from home when he was quite young — some problem at school, I gathered — and gone to London. About the time I was born he paid her a visit, but from what she told me, it was only to say he was well and she needn't worry. After that, about all they did was exchange Christmas cards. Just before she died in 1917, my mother wrote to him and asked him to take care of me. God bless him, he did — he sent me to school and when I got out he gave me an allowance and tried to get me jobs, and every now and then he called me a hopeless wastrel and threatened to cut me off with a shilling." Muirdyke dabbed at his eyes with a handkerchief.

Edwina was sorrier than ever for her flippancy. To cover up her embarrassment she made a snowball and flung it at a nearby tree, missing it by a yard. Muirdyke followed suit and hit the tree dead center.

"I never was good at games," said Edwina. "At school, I was the one who was always picked last for a side. Then I found out I could draw, so I worked hard at that, until I was better than any of the others."

"I got along with my schoolfellows," replied Charles. "The masters, on the other hand…"

They walked on for a while in silence.

"So you're here to paint Uncle Sebastian," said Muirdyke. "I don't know how you artists do it. Is it your job, or just something you like to do?"

"Both, actually," said Edwina. "It *is* my job, or, at least, how I earn my living; but I often paint or sketch for my own enjoyment, and also for practise."

"I've sometimes wondered how one goes about becoming a

painter," said Muirdyke. "One reads about young men going off to Paris and carrying on with models —"

"I wouldn't know about that," said Edwina. "I'm young, but I'm not a man, I've never been to Paris, and I've certainly never carried on with a model — of either sex. After my parents died —"

"I am sorry," said Muirdyke.

"It happened some time ago. They were killed when our house caught fire and burned to the ground. I was away visiting my aunt in London or I should likely have died too. I was only sixteen at the time, so I stayed on with her. They didn't leave much; but they had insured their lives, so I had a bit of capital. I'd always wanted to be a painter and began taking lessons at a studio. After a few years I started painting portraits for friends, and then for friends of friends, and I've built up a bit of a reputation as someone who can do good work at reasonable rates. Your uncle was my biggest commission yet. I think I can finish the portrait, but I don't know if the *Panopticon* will still want it."

"If they don't, I should like it for myself — that is, if Uncle Sebastian *hasn't* cut me off with a shilling."

"What will you do if he has? Oh, that's right, you have a job now."

"How do you know that?"

Edwina blushed. "I'm afraid I was eavesdropping on the inspector," she said. "Irrepressible curiosity."

"How to investigate a murder and all that sort of thing?"

"Yes. I hope you don't mind."

"Good Lord, no. I've always wondered how it was done… I say! I've read a lot of thrillers. There's almost always a young man and woman mixed up in the case and they solve it before the police do. Why don't we give it a try?"

Edwina shook her head. "I think the inspector would be horribly annoyed."

"It's just as well," said Muirdyke with a regretful sigh. "Can't work and detect at the same time; if I tried I'd be out on my ear…*again.*"

Edwina picked up on the emphasis. "You have trouble keeping jobs?"

"Oh, Lord, yes. I suppose it's my fault, really. I try — but something always comes up. I go out for something and run into a pal and have to stop in at a pub and pass the time of day — or there's a pretty young thing in the office to chat up — or I've been out the night before and show up late with a headache — or it's a fine day and the nags are running somewhere. I really can't blame them. Even when I buckle down and try… Look, do *you* know the difference between a debit and a credit?"

"No."

"That's what got me the boot the last time. I even got a book about accountancy, but it was double-Dutch to me. I think wines and spirits will be more in my line."

"That I can believe. Oh, dear — sorry, I did it again."

"Did what?"

"Spoke before thinking."

"Oh, *I* don't mind. Well, here we are."

The whitewashed exterior of the Green Wyvern made the public house look as if it were built of the snow lying about it. Within, firelight gleamed on the polished oak settles and tables and the bottles and pewter tankards behind the bar.

The pub was busier than might have been expected on a weekday morning, as several of Minstrel Folly's inhabitants had stopped in for refreshment after shoveling snow. The talk was all of Oldfield's demise. Constable Higgins had gone to bed as soon as he was dropped off at the station, but the nighttime telephone operator was the daughter of the Wyvern's landlord and had listened in to the call.

"All I can say is, I'm not surprised," said a stout, red-faced man. "They're strange folk, up at the Manor."

"True enough, Tom," agreed his crony, even stouter and redder. "Six years, almost, since they came here, and who's seen Mr. Oldfield in those six years? Nobody. And nobody visits him."

"Not like it was in Sir Cholmondeley's time," said Tom. "Comings and goings all the time —"

"And goings-on, too," said his crony with a guffaw. "Drinking and gaming. And the ladies."

"Ladies, indeed," sniffed the barmaid, a plump, black-haired, black-eyed young woman named Doris. "None of them any better than they should have been. Say whatever you like about Mr. Oldfield, but at least he behaved himself."

"And none of the servants allowed in the Wyvern," continued Tom. "Not since that footman — what was his name?"

"James," said a thin young man, who kept a garage. "James Jackson."

"That's right, Will," said Tom. "Jackson it was. He blabbed a bit too much about what was going on in Mr. Oldfield's workshop. As soon as Mr. Oldfield got word of it, out the door he was with a month's wages and no character."

"That wasn't Mr. Oldfield that did that," put in Joe Bulwer, land-lord of the pub. "That was Mr. Cabell, Jackson said."

"That's right," said an elderly man named Dandridge, once the postman, now retired. His wife was still the postmistress. "And a couple of days later Mr. Muirdyke came from the manor with a cheque from Mr. Oldfield for fifty pounds and asked me to send it on to Jackson."

"I saw Mr. Oldfield," said Will. "Once. I took Mr. Muirdyke's car up after he'd run it into the post office. Mr. Oldfield was in the rose garden. Didn't see anything odd about him. Waved to me and shouted hullo."

"I remember that time," said Dandridge. "Took ten years off Mrs. Dandridge's life, it did. Still, Mr. Muirdyke did the handsome thing and apologised the next day, and Mr. Oldfield paid to have the post office repaired."

"Mr. Oldfield won't be missed, anyhow," said Tom. "You can't miss what you never knew."

"That depends on who's the new owner," said Joe. "And you can't deny Minstrel Folly is the better for him being here. It wasn't just the post office. Who paid for the new village school? And for repairing the church after the fire in '25? And had the roads paved? If Sir Cholmondeley hadn't sold the manor we'd still be in mud up to our knees."

"And why shouldn't he?" asked Tom's crony. "He was rich enough. Probably killed for his money."

"Who gets it?" asked Tom.

"Who knows?" replied the crony. "I'm sure none of *us* will."

"I hope it isn't that Mr. Cabell," said Dandridge. "Remember last summer when he came down and made such a row over a parcel that had gone missing? He as good as accused Mrs. Dandridge of stealing it. Ice-cold he was, too, for all he was so angry."

"Mr. Muirdyke, perhaps," said Will. "He'd be all right."

"It was Bolshies that did it," interjected Harris, the elderly sexton. "Always after secrets, the Bolshies are, and everybody knows there are a powerful lot of secrets up at the manor."

"You've got Bolshies on the brain, Ned Harris," said Tom. "Remember when Mrs. Larbreth's cows stopped giving? You blamed *that* on the Bolshies when it was really mouldy feed."

"Will's right," said Dandridge. "The village wouldn't have reason to complain if the manor goes to Mr. Muirdyke. Remember when I was laid up last August? He was stopping there at the time and every day he came down to deliver the post, until Jimmy Burke came along to take over the job."

"Aye," said Joe Bulwer. "Came into the Wyvern that day with you and Jimmy and stood drinks all round — said it was to celebrate the first time he'd resigned from a job instead of getting sacked."

The talk stopped when Muirdyke and Edwina entered.

Muirdyke greeted the landlord. "Morning, Joe. I see everyone's been hard at work. Dashed great storm, wasn't it? Joe, meet Miss Hackett. Miss Hackett — Joe Bulwer, the landlord. A pint of Folly ale for me, Joe, and a half for the lady. Brews it himself, Miss Hackett, and dashed well."

"Good morning, Mr. Charles," said Joe, drawing the ale, "and pleased to meet you, Miss Hackett. May I say, Mr. Charles, how sorry we all are to hear of your uncle's death?"

Before Muirdyke could reply, a sour-faced old man sitting alone in a corner remarked in an ill-tempered tone to no one in particular, "Nay, not all. So that old — — got his head knocked in last night? Serves him right, the — — ."

"Oh, it does, does it?" said Muirdyke. "And perhaps, Silas Painter, you could tell us why it served him right?"

"There be no need to," replied Painter. "The whole village knows what he did — aye, and what he was doing. And if it isn't stopped, Mr. Sneering Nephew, somebody else'll likely come to a bad end too."

"That's enough, Grandad!" cried Doris. "Anybody'd think Mr. Oldfield pushed you out in the snow to starve on Christmas Eve, instead of moving you out of that tumbledown old cottage and into a nice little house in the village, warm and dry and close to your kin — *and* to the pub."

"That there cottage and that there bit of land was Painter's cottage and Painter's land time out of mind," said the old man, "mine and my Dad's afore me, aye, and my Grandad's, and *his* dad's afore him."

"And not a one of you did more with it than 'ud keep you in beer," said Doris. "It's a good thing there's no more Painters after you, just Mum, who had the sense to marry an honest, hard-working man. Now get along home — not yet noon and you drunk already!"

Painter rose from the corner where he had been sitting and, leaning on his cane — a remarkably handsome stick of polished wood with an ornate silver handle — began limping slowly to the door. Before he reached it, Edwina spoke.

"How did you know he was killed by a blow to the head, Mr. Painter?" she asked.

Painter stopped and turned. "Eh?" he answered. "Was he? I didn't know."

"Then why did you say 'knocked on the head?'"

"All I meant was he's killed and dead, the — — ," said Painter, and spat on the floor at Edwina's feet.

"OUT!" shouted Doris. Two other men in the bar came up and, taking hold of Painter, politely but firmly escorted him out the door.

"That filthy old…blighter!" said Muirdyke, red-faced with anger. "Dash it, I ought to have kicked him into the street! In fact —" He made as if to go out after Painter.

Edwina took hold of his arm. "No you oughtn't," she said. "Not a drunken, lame old man."

"Oh, don't mind him," said Doris. "He's my grandad, but he's a tiresome piece of work all the same."

"That he is, Miss," said Joe the landlord, "though I've rarely seen him as bad as today. Tell you what, have another, on the house, and you too, Mr. Charles."

Muirdyke accepted the peace offering but Edwina demurred. "Thanks, Joe, but one's my limit," she said. "Just a lemon squash."

"Certainly, Miss," said Joe, to whom Edwina was welcome as Mr. Charles's lady friend.

"So what *did* my uncle do?" asked Muirdyke, sipping his second pint.

"Well, Mr. Charles," began Joe. "Silas Painter lived in this old cottage on the manor with its bit of land and took little enough care of either. Mr. Oldfield wanted some land to do experimenting with and there was Painter's bit right to hand. So Mr. Oldfield fixed up a house here in the village — you'd think it was brand-new when it was done — and moved Silas into it, and Silas lives there now, rent-free. But he didn't want to be moved and he hasn't got over it."

"And what was my uncle doing that Painter's so upset about?"

"To tell the truth, Mr. Charles, nobody rightly knows, but Silas will have it he's been poisoning that land."

"I'll tackle Cabell when he gets back," said Muirdyke, "and get to the bottom of this." He finished his ale, arranged with Joe to have his luggage brought up to the manor, and he and Edwina started back for lunch. As they neared the house, a car came racing up the drive and stopped at the front door. A man jumped out and striding rapidly, almost running, entered the house. The driver leisurely emerged, took two suitcases from the boot and carried them into the house, returned, and drove away.

"I say," said Muirdyke, "Cabell's back."

6

SEBASTIAN OLDFIELD WAS A RARE GENIUS

Mallow and his colleagues had not got very far in their examination of the papers when a tall, thin man of about forty burst in and announced, "I'm John Cabell. Which of you is the inspector? What are you doing in Mr. Oldfield's workshop?"

For what seemed to Mallow the fiftieth time that day, he introduced himself. "I'm here investigating Mr. Oldfield's murder, of which I believe you have been informed."

"I'm sorry. This is a dreadful business," said Cabell, collecting himself. He removed his hat to reveal a full head of black hair. Below black brows his dark-blue eyes, alert and watchful, radiated a keen intelligence. "A dreadful business," he repeated. "Sebastian Oldfield was a rare genius — a true polymath. Only fifty years old and at the height of his powers — what benefits has the world lost by his untimely death? Who could have wanted to kill him?"

"I hope you understand that we must search this workshop thoroughly, including these two offices and any papers in them. I have a search-warrant, if you wish to see it."

"Oh! Then...certainly," answered Cabell. "And I wish you joy of the search. Mr. Oldfield didn't keep notes but — as you can see — I do. If you will permit, I'll stay here to answer questions, and to ensure the papers are put back pretty much as they are. I must also be present during the search of the workrooms so you and your men don't inadvertently injure any of the apparatus; or yourselves — some of it is dangerous if handled unwarily."

"You may remain. First — this is strictly routine — can you please give an account of your movements yesterday evening?"

"Of course," said Cabell. "Mr. Oldfield and I worked until about five o'clock. Then he went away to sit for Miss Hackett. I came up to the house with him and went to my room and packed. I left at about seven to drive to Fenchester to take the 8:55 to London — I left early because of the snow. A good thing too — as it was, I nearly missed the train. The roads were appalling."

"What was the purpose of your journey to London?"

"Mr. Oldfield required some gold for a new kind of accumulator he was developing. He had an arrangement with a London jeweler — Crosby and Sons — to furnish him with small quantities of precious metals as needed for his experiments. I went to London intending to pick it up today."

"How small a quantity was it?"

"One troy ounce — a little over thirty grams."

"That's not very much. Couldn't it have been sent by post?"

"It was, at first. Then, last August, the metal didn't arrive — lost or stolen *en route.* After that, Mr. Oldfield decided I should go to London and bring it back personally."

"I see. Now, you were Mr. Oldfield's secretary and assistant. How long have you worked for him?"

"Is this relevant, Inspector?"

"When a man is murdered, everything about him is potentially relevant."

"I defer to your judgment." Cabell removed an untidy pile of paper from a chair and sat down. He leaned back, closed his eyes, and began. "I have been with Mr. Oldfield from the beginning. I had just come over from Canada — this was in the spring of 1913 — and met him purely by chance. He mentioned he was looking for a technical assistant — he was working on his first successful invention, an unbreakable glass. I offered myself for the job and he took me on.

"Mr. Oldfield patented his unbreakable glass later that year, but lacked the resources to exploit it. He leased the patent to — I believe it was Caltrop Glassworks at the time — and it took off like a rocket. On the strength of the royalties he was receiving he was able to raise enough capital to continue with his experiments.

"Then the War broke out and he had his hands full with war work. I was a great help to him then — he couldn't possibly have done it by himself. We moved from London to Fenshire in 1915 to escape the Zeppelin raids and stayed on after the War ended, as it was cheaper than London but still conveniently near. We bought a house in Swannington, which served as both a residence and a business office, and acquired an old warehouse, which we converted into a workshop.

"Mr. Oldfield's experiments and inventions continued to be successful, and he prospered. When he heard in 1921 that Minstrel Manor was up for sale he decided to buy it — chiefly because it had one of the finest rose gardens in England. In passing, may I say that under Mr. Oldfield's stewardship the gardens have become even finer. We added the wings and this workshop and have lived here ever since."

From somewhere, three chimes sounded. Mallow looked about but could not see the source. "A reminder," said Cabell, and rose. "Have you any more questions, Inspector?"

"Yes," replied Mallow.

"Would you mind coming with me?" Cabell left his office. Mallow and Pyke followed him to the room of plants and animals. As they talked, Cabell moved from plant to plant, watering them. Some of the plants had small notebooks and coloured glass phials standing beside their pots; at each of these, before watering, he added a measured quantity of liquid or powder from its phial to the soil and made a note in the book.

"The workshop in Swannington," said Mallow. "Is it still in operation?"

"Yes. This one is only for research and experimentation. The other one is our main shop, where we turn our ideas into reality and see if they work. You wish to see it?"

"I do."

"I'll ring up the manager — his name is Bob Attkinson — and tell him to expect you."

"Do you know if anyone bore Mr. Oldfield a grudge — a business rival he had worsted, or an associate who thought he had done him down, or an employee who thought he had been treated unfairly — anything like that?"

Cabell paused in his activities and considered this. Finally he said, "No. Mr. Oldfield was an honest man and a just employer. No one had any reason to complain of ill-treatment at his hands."

"What about the servants here?"

"All of them have been here since we purchased the manor. They had been in the service of Sir Cholmondeley Maunder, the previous owner, and we kept them on. Except Pembert — Sir Cholmondeley's butler wished to retire, so we found Pembert to replace him."

"How did this come about?"

"Pembert was recommended to us by Howard Draven, the soap manufacturer, with whom we were having some dealings."

"What sort of dealings?"

"Nothing of great moment — we were working with him to devise improved methods of adding various scents to the soap."

"I understand there were some differences between Mr. Oldfield and his nephew. Can you shed any light on them?"

"I should not go so far as even to call them differences, Inspector. Charles Muirdyke, although twenty-four, is in some ways not quite grown up. Mr. Oldfield often expressed his concern about this, and urged his nephew to be more responsible, but never in an ill-tempered way, and Muirdyke took it in good part. There was great affection between them."

"And what was there between him and you?"

"Mr. Oldfield was not perfect — he could be quite testy and impatient with anyone, including me, who could not keep pace with his thoughts. But that never amounted to much. As for myself, I had a great admiration for him."

"Had Mr. Oldfield received any threats — by letter or otherwise?"

"No — never."

"I have received information about Mr. Oldfield's daily routine." Mallow related what he had learned from Pembert. "Can you confirm or add to this?"

"No — what you have been told is quite accurate."

"For a successful inventor, he seems to have spent very little time inventing."

"He did almost all his work in his head, Inspector. His hobbies were not just for relaxation; he said they occupied his conscious mind, freeing his unconscious mind to solve problems or come up with new ideas." Cabell reached the last plant and watered it. He moved on to a cage of mice. "*Would* you be so kind, Inspector?" he asked, handing Mallow a large box. "I'd ask your assistant, but he's busy noting down my answers."

"He had a curious collection of hobbies," resumed Mallow. Cabell opened the cage, took out the mice, and put them in the box. "Roses, model railways, cards —"

"How did you deduce — oh, of course, you would have found them in your searches. Yes, he played Patience a great deal." Cabell took the cage to a corner of the room and emptied out the litter into a bin. The scent of ammonia drifted across the room.

"And theology."

"*Theology?*" Cabell laughed. "Where on earth did you get that idea?" He wiped the bottom of the cage with some cotton waste and covered it with fresh litter from a large bag.

"There were quite a number of books in the library —"

"Oh, those. They came with the manor. Sir Cholmondeley was greatly in debt; that was why he sold the manor. Before doing so, he auctioned off its contents. No one wanted those books." Cabell returned with the cage and put the mice back in. He went to the next cage, removed two guinea pigs, and placed them in the box.

"Speaking of books — what was the purpose of the dummy books in the study?"

"The set of dummy books is actually a safe. Mr. Oldfield patented the idea and has in fact sold several of them. He never actually used it, though. It was enough for him to have it."

"He had no notes or papers that needed to be kept secret?"

"You have made a study of detective fiction, Inspector. No, I'm sorry to say, we have not been inventing submarines, aero-torpedoes, or death-rays here."

"Just in case — can you open it?"

"No. Only Mr. Oldfield knew the combination."

"I see. Now, there is some question about how the murderer entered and left Mr. Oldfield's study. For someone who, I have been told, was something of a recluse, there are a remarkable number of ways in which someone could get to him. The passage door — that is a very curious door. I understand only you, Pembert, and Mr. Oldfield had keys to it."

"That is correct."

"Could a copy have been made?"

"Absolutely not, unless by Mr. Oldfield or myself. An ordinary locksmith wouldn't have the slightest idea of the principle on which the key works."

"I see. By the way, I must ask you for your key." Cabell took a bunch of keys from his pocket and removed the one to the study door. He made to give it to Mallow, who was still holding the box, now occupied by a rabbit, and handed it to Pyke instead. "Now, what about the keys to the French window and the staircase?" continued the inspector.

"Only Mr. Oldfield had those. Of course, those were ordinary keys and could be copied; but they were always on his person."

"And the door into the library. What was the purpose of that?"

Cabell laughed again. "I must explain to you, Inspector, that Mr. Oldfield, like his nephew, had a boyish streak — as you could see from his model railway. When we added the new wings to the manor, shortly after we purchased it, Mr. Oldfield insisted on having a secret door. I don't know that he used it much, if at all — again, just having it was enough."

"How many people knew of the door?"

"Everyone in the manor. Mr. Oldfield made no secret of it."

"Including Charles Muirdyke?"

"Oh, yes. He enjoyed using it when he was younger." They had reached a cage with a snake in it. Mallow had a horror of snakes. He handed the box to Pyke in exchange for the constable's notebook and pencil. Cabell smiled but made no comment.

"And are there any other means of — well — surreptitious entry?" asked Mallow.

"I'm afraid not, Inspector."

"Another thing. Mr. Oldfield left a dying message — we found it on a piece of paper under his body. I've made a copy. As you were close to him, perhaps you can interpret it." Mallow set down Pyke's notebook, took out his own, opened it to the page where he had written *"justis lik tortis,"* and showed it to Cabell.

Cabell studied it carefully. His frown of concentration gradually gave way to a look of puzzlement. Finally he said, "I'm sorry, but the message says nothing to me. I expect he was delirious when he wrote it."

"Thank you," said Mallow. "We'll have to see what the experts make of the original. While I think of it — who is Mr. Oldfield's solicitor? The contents of his will may throw some light on his murder."

"Henry Radford," replied Cabell, "of Banks & Radford, in Swannington."

"Excellent — is there an outside telephone here? As he is the coroner, I should ring him up anyway to arrange for the inquest."

"Yes. Come along, please." They returned to Cabell's office. "Let me assist you — the telephone system here at the manor is Mr. Oldfield's own invention and not very clear to anyone unused to it."

With Cabell's assistance, Mallow got through to Henry Radford. He informed the lawyer of Oldfield's murder and asked for an inquest to be arranged as quickly as possible; he also appointed a time the following morning to meet with Mr. Radford to review the will.

"Before I forget," said Mallow, "Constable Pyke will have to take your fingerprints."

"Happy to oblige."

While the fingerprinting was going on, Cabell caught sight of Porlock looking through the notebook of experiments. He cried out "Hoy!" and, without waiting for Pyke to clean the ink off his fingers, strode over and snatched the book away.

"I say!" remarked the constable in surprise.

"I beg your pardon," said Cabell. "The contents of this book are confidential in the highest degree. We are not the only ones working in some areas and the information would be of immense value to our rivals."

"Oh, yes? Submarines, aero-torpedoes, or death-rays?" asked Mallow, annoyed at the affront to his subordinate.

With a visible effort Cabell controlled himself. "No, Inspector. Just things of commercial value."

"You can trust us to keep the information confidential," said Mallow. "We are merely interested in it as it may relate to Mr. Oldfield's murder."

"Then you don't need it," replied Cabell. "The notebook is mine, for my use. Mr. Oldfield had no need for notes or plans." He tapped his forehead. "He kept everything up there. He had a phenomenal memory — he could read an article in the Encyclopaedia Britannica once and six months later repeat it word for word."

"Nevertheless, we must examine it." Mallow paused in thought for a moment. "Perhaps we can compromise. Constable Porlock will finish going through the book; you can review the notes he takes and strike out anything you don't want revealed."

"That will be acceptable."

But, as it turned out, Porlock found nothing worth noting. In the end, the only items of possible significance they came upon were several bundles of canceled cheques and a ledger. These Mallow kept, promising Cabell they would be returned.

Mallow and his colleagues returned to the house to take leave before returning to Fenchester. Edwina and Muirdyke were waiting for him.

"There's someone in the village you need to speak to," Edwina informed him.

"A dashed nasty old man named Silas Painter," added Muirdyke.

"He may know something about the murder — at any rate, he certainly had a grudge against Mr. Oldfield," said Edwina. "He lives in the village — I don't know which house, but you can ask his granddaughter — she works in the pub."

"You'll have to wait, though," said Muirdyke, "he's tight as an owl now."

"Thank you. I'll speak with him tomorrow. We must get back to headquarters, so I'll take my leave now. I must ask that neither of you leaves the neighbourhood for the time being."

"Of course. I was planning to stay a few days anyway. Dashed interesting meeting you, Inspector," replied Muirdyke.

"Likewise," added Edwina with a friendly grin, which Mallow did not return.

"I don't think the inspector likes me," said Edwina, mock-mournfully, as the police drove off.

"More fool he," replied Muirdyke.

7

WHO, WHAT, WHEN, WHERE, WHY, AND HOW

During the drive back to Fenchester, Mallow dozed while Bellman went over Pyke's shorthand notes of the interviews with Pembert, William, Edwina, Muirdyke, and Cabell.

Fenchester, once subordinate to Chiltonbury, had in the past century surpassed the latter and was now the chief municipality of Fenshire. It was a town devoted to commerce. Warehouses and wharves lined the River Culver, wholesale dealers in woollen goods and china, tea and tobacco, fancy goods and lace, and innumerable other commodities could be found throughout, and the Bank of Fenshire was one of the largest in the Midlands. The smoke belching from mills and factories covered all with layer on layer of soot.

At police headquarters — a mid-Victorian hodgepodge of no architectural merit whatever — Mallow and his subordinates gathered in his office for a conference. The room had little character yet, having been granted to Mallow upon his promotion. On a wall was a map of Fenshire; the few shelves were bare save for a police manual, a railway guide, and two marksmanship trophies from the East Fenshire Rifle Club.

Before the meeting opened, Mallow sent Pyke to take the fingerprints of the household to Sergeant Henley for comparison with those found in the study, and Porlock to make a fresh pot of coffee.

Bellman took out his pipe, hesitated, and looked at Mallow.

"Go ahead," said the inspector. Bellman filled his pipe and began looking in his pockets for matches.

"Let's have a talk before I fall asleep," began Mallow when the constables had returned. "We're here, not to theorise ahead of our data, but to take a preliminary survey, as it were, which may give us ideas of where to look first, without jumping to conclusions. We'll start with — what do we start with, Pyke?"

"Coffee, sir," answered Pyke, handing the inspector a cup.

"A point to you," replied Mallow. "But what else?"

"Who, What, When, Where, Why, and How."

"Right. The What is clear enough: we're investigating the murder of one Sebastian Oldfield. I think it's safe to say murder — one doesn't commit suicide by bashing one's own skull in with a paperweight, nor does such a thing happen by accident. The How is also clear — yes, Pyke?" Pyke had raised his hand.

"Excuse me, sir, but I don't think we can say it is. We saw the wound, and we saw a paperweight with blood on it. Are the two *necessarily* related?"

Bellman paused in the act of lighting his pipe long enough to say, "That's enough, Pyke."

"No, Pyke is quite right," said Mallow. "Conceivably the murderer wanted to lay a false trail. In that case he would have taken the real weapon away with him and we may never find it."

"Why would the murderer want to do that?" asked Porlock.

"Because the real weapon was one that was more or less obviously connected with him," said Mallow. "In which case, perhaps its absence will be noticed. Meanwhile, let's hope the post-mortem shows it *was* the paperweight. Moving on, can we agree on the Where?"

"No, sir," said Bellman. He glared at Pyke. "If we're going to question what we've seen with our own eyes, we can't say *positively*

Oldfield was killed in the study. He might have been killed elsewhere and the body moved."

"Very good, Bellman," said Mallow, grinning. "You're getting into the spirit of the thing. Porlock!"

"Me, sir?" answered Porlock, taken by surprise.

"What does that leave?"

The constable did not answer at once. Finally he got out, "Who, When, and Why."

"Why depends on Who," said Mallow. "In fact, Why is the least important question. People commit murder for the seemingly most absurd reasons. Next comes When. It's pretty clear Oldfield was killed shortly before ten. That fits in with Dr. Melmoth's estimate and also Pembert's testimony that the body was still warm — unless Pyke has an objection?"

"No, sir — only there is an inconsistency with the rigor."

"As the doctor said, rigor's a chancy thing. The post-mortem should clear it up."

"Leaving us with Who," said Bellman. "Accepting the time of death, the obvious suspects are Pembert and Miss Hackett. And of the two, I'd put my money on Pembert. Miss Hackett said she didn't see anyone come along the passage but him. If she did it, surely she'd have said that she dozed, or left the library for a time."

"But if Pembert did it," argued Pyke, "why should he have said the body was still warm? The other servants give him an alibi right up to when he brought the whisky-and-soda to the study. And Miss Hackett says she didn't hear anything."

"How much noise does hitting someone over the head with a brass dragon make?" asked Mallow. "It's not exactly the sort of thing one can test by experiment. Now, outside the house we have to look at Charles Muirdyke and this Painter fellow. Cabell was well on his way to London at ten and can be ruled out. Finally, there's X."

"X, sir?" asked Pyke and Porlock together.

"X — the unknown. Someone of whose existence we are not yet aware."

"I see, sir," said Pyke.

"We're not done yet. We must consider Who in the light of the larger How and When. How did the murderer enter and leave the study? Taking the ways in order: first, the door to the passage. Either the murderer had a key, or Oldfield admitted him. Only Oldfield, Cabell, and Pembert had keys. If the murderer left through the door, he must have had a key."

"How do you see that?" asked Bellman.

"Because the button on Oldfield's desk opens the door and leaves it open. You have to press it again to close the door. The murderer wouldn't have time to get out before the door closed."

Pyke raised his hand again. "He could have blocked the door from fully closing with a book or something."

"True," said Mallow. "We'll have to go back and see if that can be done. What about the French window?"

"Locked," said Bellman. "And Oldfield had the key. Also, it was snowing pretty hard by seven; it may not have been possible to open the window. And one more thing — if it *was* opened, snow would have blown in, or been tracked in by the murderer; yet the carpet was perfectly dry."

"Rate the window possible but improbable," pronounced Mallow. "Next — the staircase door. Anyone with a key — and it was an ordinary key, easily copied — could have come and gone."

"Except for the boxes," reminded Bellman.

"Yes, the boxes," agreed Mallow. "I don't like them. They have a whiff of red herring about them. Why were they in such an inconvenient place? Why not in a corner, or under the railway table? Finally — the concealed door. Damn Oldfield and his 'boyish streak.' Why did he have to complicate things?"

"If that was the way taken, then Miss Hackett is involved," said Pyke. "She was in the library the whole time."

"She *said* she was," Bellman pointed out.

"Then if she wasn't in the library the whole time, the concealed door wasn't used," said Porlock.

"That doesn't follow," replied Pyke. "Now, if we presume Pembert and Miss Hackett are both telling the truth, then it was X, through the window or the staircase."

"And if one of them isn't?" asked Bellman.

"We're getting ahead of ourselves," said Mallow. He yawned. "Is there any coffee left? No? Blast. Well, I think we've covered all we can, pending further information — oh, wait. Did you find anything in the servants' quarters, Bellman?"

"Nothing out of the ordinary."

"What about the cellars?"

"Nothing there either, except machinery."

"It sounds like we have a lot of work ahead of us, sir," said Pyke.

"Yes, we do. We must ask every question that occurs to us, and when the answers give rise to further questions, we must ask them too. Eventually, God willing, we'll have enough pieces to complete the jigsaw." Mallow yawned again and fell into a half-doze. The others continued the discussion in lowered tones.

"Pembert at ten along the passage," said Porlock. "Miss Hackett at any time between seven and ten along the passage or through the concealed door, or anybody through the window or the staircase."

"If it was Miss Hackett, then not at any time," said Pyke. "She would have to have killed Oldfield shortly before ten."

"How do you read that?"

"Because according to Pembert the body was still warm when he found it, meaning the murder had just taken place."

"That's a point for Pembert," said Porlock. "If he did it, why would he mention something that pointed to himself?"

Bellman sighed. "We talked about that before, Porlock. Weren't you listening?"

"Sorry... How reliable is Miss Hackett? Could she have dozed, or moved from her chair, or left the library, and didn't say so because it slipped her memory?"

"Possibly," replied Bellman. "I don't trust her. She comes across as flighty, but there's a brain behind it. Her behaviour over the concealed door is suspicious. She knew how to open it from the library side."

"She told us she asked Pembert," put in Pyke.

"She *told* us," replied Bellman. "And in the study — do you remember how she made a dash for the door? Now if we find her fingerprints on the panel — *or* on the other side — she has a perfectly innocent explanation for how they got there."

"Is she the criminal, or an accomplice?" asked Pyke. "If she's an accomplice, that could explain why she went into the study after the body was found. She said it was curiosity; but she could have wanted to do any amount of cleaning up or rearranging to throw us off the scent. Take the boxes — she could have replaced them."

"But why tell us she went in?" asked Porlock.

"Because Pembert saw her."

"In that case, Pembert's out of it. But then, why go in from the passage? Why not from the library?"

"She may *not* have known about the door. I don't like the idea of rearranging the boxes. Pembert had already been in the study. Very likely he'd remember where they had been."

"Could she and Pembert be working together?" asked Porlock.

"Unlikely," said Bellman. "If they were, their stories would fit together. Pembert finds the body; Miss Hackett dozed, or moved from her chair, or left the library, or even closed the door — we only have her word for it she's claustrophobic."

"Is there anything else?" asked Pyke. "The trains, or the books — and I'll bet five shillings there's something in that safe, whatever Cabell says. Secret papers, maybe."

"Did anybody look in the boxes?" asked Porlock.

"They were closed and taped," said Bellman.

"The Inspector's right," said Pyke. "We're getting ahead —"

He was interrupted by Mallow who suddenly sat up and exclaimed "Paper!"

"What?" asked Bellman.

"Those fragments of paper you found. Pembert told us Oldfield cleaned the study every morning. The paper had to have come there the day of the murder."

"But does that make them a clue? Oldfield might have torn something up."

"Would a man so finicky about cleaning leave bits of paper lying about the floor? He could have; but the odds are it was the murderer. We'll have to go back to the manor tomorrow. We'll see if we can find where they came from." Mallow yawned again. "But for now, you can go. I'm done in."

When he was alone, Mallow removed his spectacles, leaned back in his chair, put his feet up on his desk, and fell instantly asleep.

The inspector jerked awake at the sound of the telephone.

"Better answer it, George," came a voice. Mallow looked about and saw the broad face of Superintendent Runciman peering around the door.

Mallow picked up the receiver. John Cabell was at the other end. "I spoke with Bob Attkinson, Inspector. You can see him tomorrow afternoon at one-thirty."

Mallow put on his spectacles and drew a piece of paper to him. "One-thirty, you said?"

"Yes." Mallow wrote it down, thanked Cabell, and hung up.

"Sleeping on the job, George?" asked Runciman. "I've sent men back to a beat along the wharves for less."

"Sorry, sir," said Mallow, getting awkwardly to his feet. "I didn't get much sleep last night."

The Superintendent's face relaxed into a smile. "I know, George. I'm the one that sent you out. Are you up to giving me a verbal report?"

"Yes, sir — may I have a minute to collect my thoughts?"

"Certainly. I'll be in my office."

Mallow visited the washroom, threw cold water on his face,

smoothed his rumpled appearance, and presented himself at Runciman's door.

"Come in, George, sit down, and sing about the unhappy lot of a policeman."

Mallow obeyed the spirit rather than the letter of that last instruction, and gave Runciman a précis of his investigations. "I should be receiving reports from Henley and Dr. Melmoth later today," he concluded. "Tomorrow I'm meeting Mr. Radford in Swannington about the inquest and Oldfield's will. There will probably be more questions to ask at the manor. Then there's that possible suspect in Minstrel Folly to vet —"

"Yes — this Painter fellow the bright young things winkled out for you. Always good to have assistance, eh?"

"They can both go to…Hull," said Mallow with feeling. "Especially the Hackett woman."

"Patience, George, patience," counseled Runciman. "By the end of the case I'm sure you'll have them both wagging their tails and eating out of your hand."

Mallow's rancour gave way to amusement at the mental picture this conjured up. "But I can't say I've met a likely suspect yet. Neither Muirdyke nor Miss Hackett strikes me as a murderer. The butler — Pembert — doesn't either."

"You can't always trust your instincts, George. Never forget that. Murderers come in all shapes and sizes, some of them very unlikely. What about Cabell?"

"He could be. Pleasant enough, but there's something cold about him. He has an alibi, though."

"Hmph. We've both seen alibis before. Is it breakable?"

"Not likely, sir. The 8:55 is the last train to London, and we know he was there because Pembert reached him at his hotel. Still, we'll inquire at the station. We'll also find out from the railway who the guard or guards were on the train and interview them."

"Always good to be thorough, George," approved Runciman. "I've spoken with the Chief Constable. He wants a written report. Think you can get one to me tomorrow?"

"Yes, sir."

"The fingerprints — have you sent copies to Scotland Yard?"

"Good Lord, no, sir. I forgot. I'll have one of the constables take them up."

Mallow returned to his office. He dispatched Constable Verner to London with the fingerprints and began drafting a report.

Sergeant Henley was the first to provide further data.

"The note was not written by an educated hand," he told the inspector. "The printing shows the characteristic signs of having been the work of a person who was illiterate, or nearly so."

"The note was not written by Oldfield?" said Mallow, surprised.

"Doesn't look that way. As to the other papers, they do appear to be an attempt by the writer to practise two people's signatures."

"Confirmation. What about prints?"

"The only fingerprints on them were Oldfield's."

"Not even smudges?"

"No. The would-be forger must have used gloves, or wiped them clean."

"Unusual forethought on his part."

"The fingerprints we did find in the study — there weren't many — were almost all those of Oldfield himself. There were a few of Pembert's, one of Cabell's, and one of Miss Hackett's."

"And she said she didn't touch anything. Where was it?"

"In one of the dried wine-drops on the desk."

Later that afternoon came Dr. Melmoth, who had finally got round to the post-mortem.

"Not much to add to what I told you last night," he said. "Oldfield died of a fractured skull. Ninety-nine percent certain the dragon paperweight was the weapon. Nature of the fatal blow — blows, actually, he was struck twice — consistent with the paperweight, which had on it not only blood, but fragments of bone and brain tissue."

"That's not just fracturing the skull," commented Mallow. "That's shattering it. Would it have taken more than normal strength? Or could a woman have done it, or an elderly man?"

"Depends. The murderer could have struck in blind rage. Couldn't rule them out. Oldfield didn't die right away but didn't live long after being struck down. Dined shortly before death: lobster, bread, asparagus, red wine. Funny —" Dr. Melmoth fancied himself to be something of an epicure. " — Should have expected white with lobster."

"What about his overall health?"

"Fit as a fiddle — that is, for your average middle-aged sedentary man. There was a scar on his right hand from a burn, probably acid. Fairly recent — four or five months ago."

"He is said to have been subject to migraine headaches recently. Can you confirm that?"

"No. There are generally no outward physical signs."

"Thank you — Wait a moment," said Mallow. "You said Oldfield died soon after eating his dinner. How soon?"

"Almost immediately," replied the doctor. "No more than fifteen minutes or so."

"If his dinner was brought to him at seven, and he died not long before ten — why did he wait nearly three hours to eat it?"

Dr. Melmoth gave Mallow a sardonic smirk. "Maybe he died just before ten and maybe he didn't."

"Eh?"

"You pays your money and you takes your choice. Body temperature says nine-thirty to ten-thirty. Rigor consistent with death sometime before seven. Lividity suggests seven-thirty or so."

"That's impossible. He can't have died three times."

"The data is what it is," retorted Dr. Melmoth. "That's all I can tell you. The rest is your problem."

Constable Verner returned late in the evening. Bellman brought him to Mallow's office. Pyke, who had stayed late to hear Verner's report, came with them.

"Scotland Yard was able to identify one set of prints, sir," reported the constable. "They belong to a forger, Alfred Phelps Pemberton. He was convicted of forgery in 1914, released from prison in 1921, and hasn't come to the attention of the police since then."

The Yard had furnished a copy of Pemberton's file, including photographs. Mallow put on his spectacles and looked into it. "By George!" he exclaimed. "Have we got a lead at last?" As if the fingerprints were not enough, the photographs showed clearly that Pemberton the forger and Pembert the butler were the same man.

"Seems open and shut to me, sir," commented Bellman. "Pembert's forging Oldfield's signature; Oldfield catches him out and confronts him with the evidence; Pembert kills him."

"That's one scenario," agreed Mallow. "One or two things, though. We found the papers with the signatures in the desk. One would expect either that Oldfield would have had them out — in which case we shouldn't have found them at all — or that Pembert would have gone through the desk."

"Lost his head —" began Pyke.

"Bosh. A man concerned enough about his own safety to kill will be concerned enough to look for the evidence that will convict him. The other thing is that Miss Hackett didn't hear anything."

"Could she have?" asked Bellman. "Both the study and library doors would have had to be open."

"They were," said Pyke.

"She did say the library door was open." Mallow leafed through

Pyke's notes. "She didn't say about the study door — no, I'm wrong, she did say it was open. Good work, Verner. You may go."

"Thank you, sir."

Mallow scanned the rest of Pemberton's file. "Odd," he commented. "Very odd. Pemberton worked in Howard Draven's office and it was Draven's name he forged. And yet Draven got him a job afterwards."

"Then Draven is either a saint or a fool," replied Bellman.

"Or both. The two aren't mutually exclusive… While I think of it — Dr. Melmoth threw quite a spanner into the works this evening." Mallow explained the doctor's report of the time, or times, of death. "Which is absurd, as Euclid used to say. I don't remember much of the geometry I learned in school, but I remember that much."

"So what do we do about it?" asked Bellman.

"Shelve it for the moment," replied Mallow. "Something may come up to explain it; or we'll solve the case some other way and the explanation will come out." *And I wish I felt as confident as I sound. This case is already a muddle. Will something come along and make it worse?*

Bellman, sensing Mallow's unease, tried to comfort him. "It's early in the case, sir — less than twenty-four hours. Maybe Pembert will make it easy and confess when we confront him."

"Thank you, Bellman."

8

ALFRED PEMBERTON AND BARNABAS MERRYWEATHER

Mallow, Sergeants Bellman and Henley, and Constable Pyke set out early the next morning. Their first stop was at Henry Radford's office in the antique, unspoiled village of Swannington. Henley waited in the car while the others went in to see the solicitor.

Mr. Radford was waiting for them — a middle-sized, sandy-haired gentleman in his late thirties, with pale grey protruding eyes set in a round foolish face. "A sad business, this," he said. "I shall be glad to assist you however I can."

"Thank you, sir," said Mallow. "We greatly appreciate it. But before we get to the will — can you explain to me Mr. Oldfield's business?"

"Certainly. It was not, strictly speaking, a business — neither a public company nor a privately-held one. Mr. Oldfield either licensed his patents in exchange for royalties or sold them outright. He also had numerous connections and earned a good income in consulting fees from manufacturers and such."

"He was doing well?"

"Quite well."

"Did he ever, to your knowledge, engage in any kind of sharp or shady practice?"

For a moment Mr. Radford's mouth writhed as though he had tasted something foul. "That is an extremely offensive question, Inspector. I would not have stayed as his solicitor had he done so."

"I'm sorry, sir. We are obliged by our profession to ask such questions. Sometimes, I regret to say, our suspicions are justified. I wish it were not so."

The lawyer's face cleared. "Very well. The answer is no: Mr. Oldfield was scrupulously honest in all his dealings."

"Thank you. Now — I should be obliged if you could inform me of the provisions of Mr. Oldfield's will."

Mr. Radford took up the document from his desk and consulted it. "Its provisions are quite simple:

"To John Cabell, £20,000; the contents of the workshop at Minstrel Manor; the workshop in Swannington; and one-half the rights to Mr. Oldfield's patents and all current and future licenses and royalties."

"How much would that amount to?"

"As to the value of the workshops and patents, I cannot say. Mr. Oldfield was making between £5,000 and £6,000 a year in royalties."

"Please go on."

"To Arthur Pembert, also known as Alfred Pemberton, with many thanks for his loyal service, £5,000 and a house in the village of Minstrel Folly whenever he should choose to retire."

"He knew, then, that Pemberton was his butler's real name?"

"Yes. He asked whether the pseudonym would invalidate the bequest. I advised him to include the legal name. I also asked him why Pembert was going under a false name. He said only that the man was trying to live down an indiscretion in his past. I strongly urged that, as his solicitor, I should be taken into his confidence, but he refused. I was tempted to ask him to find another solicitor, but when I consulted my partner Banks, he told me not to be a — that is, he informed me it would not be necessary."

"And the rest?"

"To each of the other servants at Minstrel Manor, £100 for each year of employment, including their time in Sir Cholmondeley Maunder's service.

"The residue to Mr. Oldfield's nephew, Charles Muirdyke, in the hope and expectation he will prove a responsible steward; to be held in trust for him until he reaches the age of thirty."

"Who are the trustees?"

"John Cabell and myself."

"How much is the residue?"

"In addition to the half share in the patents, royalties, and licenses, the residue comprises Minstrel Manor, its contents and grounds, and Mr. Oldfield's personal fortune which, after all other legacies and duties have been paid, will amount to £150,000, more or less."

"That's quite a fortune."

"It is. Now, I should add, last week — I believe it was Friday — Mr. Oldfield rang me up and directed me to change his will. He wished to remove the trustees and leave the estate to Mr. Muirdyke absolutely. He also asked me to draw up a power of attorney for Mr. Muirdyke. I remonstrated with Mr. Oldfield — I am not unfamiliar with Mr. Muirdyke's character — but he insisted."

"A power of attorney for Mr. Muirdyke — he wished to be able to manage his nephew's affairs?"

"No. He wished his nephew to be able to manage *his* affairs."

That was a surprise. Mallow had seen little about Muirdyke to indicate that he was fit for such responsibility.

"Did he give any reasons?"

"No, he did not."

"Were any of the chief legatees aware of the provisions of the will?"

Again a momentary bad-taste expression crossed Mr. Radford's face. "It would have been most inappropriate for me to discuss the contents of Mr. Oldfield's testamentary dispositions with any of the legatees."

"I beg your pardon, sir. I did not mean to imply you had done so. Mr. Oldfield might have said something —"

"He did not."

"I see, sir. I have no other questions about the will at this time. About the inquest —"

"It will take place tomorrow afternoon at four o'clock, in Minstrel Folly. Who will you be calling as witnesses?"

Mallow had not expected this question. After some thought he replied, "Charles Muirdyke for evidence of identity, and Dr. Melmoth — the police surgeon — for the medical evidence. We may have questions for other persons at the manor: John Cabell, Edwina Hackett, Pembert, and William Simms."

"Who is William Simms?" asked Mr. Radford, busily writing down the names.

"One of the footmen. Also Constable Higgins, who mans the police station at Minstrel Folly."

"What sort of questions?"

"I don't know yet, sir. Pembert found the body, and reported it to Higgins, who carried out the initial investigation. Miss Hackett was in a sense present when the body was discovered."

"Who is she?"

"Miss Hackett is a professional portrait painter, engaged to paint Mr. Oldfield."

"I shall see the summonses are sent out. No doubt we will get to the bottom of this murder."

"Thank you, sir." Mallow rose.

"Before you go, Inspector —"

"Yes?" replied Mallow, seating himself again.

"I felt it due to my position as Mr. Oldfield's legal representative —" began Mr. Radford. Mallow had never heard a voice so officious and self-satisfied. "— To attempt to acquaint myself with the nature of Alfred Pemberton's 'indiscretion.' My quest met with success. In 1914 —"

"Ahem," said Mallow, raising his hand. Mr. Radford grimaced at the interruption. "We are already aware of Pembert's past, sir."

"Oh, very well. Good day to you."

Out in the street, Bellman remarked, "Why a power of attorney?

Was he planning to go away, to some place remote enough that he couldn't stay on top of things? And why Muirdyke? Cabell was already managing his day-to-day business."

"Only God and Oldfield know, and neither is talking," replied Mallow. "Changing the will makes sense, though — no point in having trustees when Oldfield is dead if Muirdyke has a free hand with his money when he's alive."

"But Oldfield died first," said Pyke. "Was he killed to keep Muirdyke from getting control of the money?"

"That's an interesting possibility," said Bellman. "Suppose Cabell has been engaging in some jiggery-pokery? Muirdyke, armed with a power of attorney, could find him out at once. As it is now, he's safe for another six years."

"You're forgetting one thing," said Mallow. "Mr. Radford is the other trustee. I think Cabell would be safer with Muirdyke than with that Nosey Parker we just left."

"Maybe Mr. Radford did it," suggested Pyke, straight-faced. "He couldn't bear the thought of Muirdyke getting his hands on Oldfield's —"

He was interrupted by a shout of laughter from Mallow. "Oh, what a thought!" the inspector exclaimed. "Pyke, you've made my day... I've half a mind to go back and ask him to account for his movements on Monday night, just to see the look on his face."

The Swannington branch of the Bank of Fenshire occupied a square Queen Anne building of considerable charm. Mallow spoke with the manager and was granted access to Oldfield's records. Their volume was dismayingly great: Oldfield's business interests were widespread and active. Looking through the most recent, he discovered a cheque written to Barnabas Merryweather in December of the previous year. The cheque was for a thousand pounds.

"So Merryweather exists," Mallow commented, "and isn't just an odd name. Have we stumbled upon X? And will we find Y or even Z waiting in the wings? I see the cheque was presented at Maunder & Co. in Chiltonbury. One more place to visit… Pyke, you stay here and go through the rest of the records."

"How far back, sir?" asked Pyke. "They start in 1915."

"All the way," replied Mallow. "You never know. The pub in Minstrel Folly — what's its name?"

"The Green Wyvern, sir," said Bellman.

"That's it. The pub won't be open yet, and we can't visit Oldfield's shop here until this afternoon; so we'll push on to the manor and have a chat with Alfred Phelps Pemberton. While we're there we can look for prints on the concealed door, and for whatever the scraps of paper came from — yes, and ask if anyone knows about this Merryweather. If you finish before we get back, Pyke, get some lunch and go for a walk. It's a fine day for a walk."

It was in fact a grey, lowering day with a hint of approaching snow; Pyke decided Superintendent Runciman's sense of humour was beginning to rub off on Mallow.

At Minstrel Manor the door was opened by Pembert himself.

"Good morning, Pembert," said Mallow. "I should like to have a word or two with you. Is there somewhere we can speak privately?"

"The drawing room is at present unoccupied," replied the butler. "I shall take you there." After sending Sergeant Henley to the study, Mallow and Bellman followed Pembert.

The drawing room was located in the other new wing. Like the rest of the manor Mallow had seen, it was neatly fitted up, with no *nouveau riche* trimmings.

"Bellman, close the door," said Mallow. "Sit down, Pembert, this should not take long."

"Yes, sir," said Pembert.

"Did Mr. Oldfield know your history?"

Pembert paled. "My — my history?"

"Yes, Pembert — or should I say, Alfred Phelps Pemberton?"

Pembert buried his face in his hands. "I knew this was coming," he groaned. "As soon as you took my fingerprints, I knew you'd find out."

"I ask again — did Mr. Oldfield know your history? And in particular, that you had been convicted of forging your employer's name to a cheque?"

"Yes, sir. I was driven to my crime. I was already in debt and then my wife and baby daughter both fell ill. They died while I was in prison. Mr. Draven — a good man, God bless him — visited me before my trial and told me I was a silly ass not to have come to him for help. He apologised for prosecuting, but it was a business matter — he owed it to his associates. At the trial he pressed for leniency. When I came out of prison in 1921, he hadn't forgot me. He sent for me and offered me the chance at a good post at Minstrel Manor, but only on condition my past must not be concealed. I accepted this and met Mr. Cabell and told him the whole story. He took me to Mr. Oldfield, to whom I repeated it. Mr. Oldfield said he was more than happy to do a good turn and took me on at once. Ask Mr. Cabell — he'll confirm everything I've said."

"I shall. Where can I find him?"

"I'm sorry, sir, but Mr. Cabell is not here. He and Miss Hackett departed some time ago in Miss Hackett's auto. I believe they were going into Fenchester."

"One other thing. Do you know anything of Mr. Oldfield's dealings with a man called Barnabas Merryweather?"

"No, I do not."

Mallow thanked the agitated Pembert and dismissed him. As the butler left, he overheard Bellman saying, "Still, we'll have to keep a close eye on him, sir."

"Of course. Let's see how Henley is getting along."

Henley had two items to report, one negative and one positive. The negative: there was only one set of prints on the concealed door. They belonged to Edwina Hackett, who, presumably, had left them when she opened the door on the previous day. The positive: he had found where the scraps of paper had come from. The pile of magazines on the reading table included a bound volume of the *Panopticon* for 1926; the August issue had been torn out.

"Good work," said Mallow. "Now, if I can remember how to use this telephone..." He eventually got through to police headquarters and Constable Porlock. "Porlock? I have a job for you. I need the August 1926 issue of the *Panopticon*. Try every newsagent in Fenchester if you have to, or the library." He looked at his watch. "Cabell's on the road and who knows when he'll be back. The pub should be open now. While we're there we can check up on Muirdyke's account of his movements Tuesday night."

Joe Bulwer confirmed the gist of Muirdyke's story. Muirdyke had had supper and then gone to his room at about eight-thirty; no one had seen him afterwards until he came down again at about a quarter to eleven. At Mallow's request, Joe showed him Muirdyke's room. Mallow observed that a short distance down the passage from the room was a back stair. Exploring it, he discovered Muirdyke could have taken the stair, left the pub by a rear door, and come back the same way, unseen by anyone.

Mallow and Bellman returned to the taproom and found Doris in her place behind the bar. Mallow introduced himself as a police officer and asked the whereabouts of Silas Painter's house.

"No need," said Doris. "Granddad's already here." She pointed out the old man, sitting in his usual corner and well into his first pint of the day; adding a facetious remark, loud enough for him to hear, about bringing the police down on them.

Mallow went over to Painter's corner. "Good morning, sir," he said, sitting down. "As your granddaughter said, I am a policeman, looking into the murder of Mr. Oldfield at Minstrel Manor. I have one or two questions I must ask you."

"*Good morning,* is it?" groused Painter, who was little better when he was sober than when he was drunk. "It'd be a sight better without you sittin' there."

"The sooner you answer my questions, the sooner I'll go," said Mallow. "I understand you had reason to dislike Mr. Oldfield?"

"Aye, so I did," said Painter, and recapitulated the complaint he had made in the presence of Muirdyke and Edwina, concluding with, "and the old — — got what he deserved."

"Very well," said Mallow when Painter was done. "Now — can you tell me what you were doing the night before last?"

"Eh? You think *I* might have done it? That's the police for you, always down on a poor old man. Well, Mr. Copper —"

"Inspector," said Bellman.

"*Inspector,* then," said Painter, giving the sergeant a malevolent glare. "Well, Mr. *Inspector,* I'll tell you anyway. I was right here until seven o'clock and then I went home and had a bit of supper and then I went to bed, and if anyone says otherwise they're a — — liar."

"Did you speak with anyone, or did anyone see you, after you left?"

"I talked to nobody. Anybody might have *seen* me, peering and prying as they are, the whole — — village."

"What about at your house?"

"Aye, Betsey was there."

"And Betsey is?"

"My daughter. Comes by every evening to cook my supper. Knows her duty to her Dad that way, even if she went off and married that Ted Mallow without my leave. And bringing up that chit of a girl —" He raised his voice. "— With no respect for her old Granddad. Nothing but sauce from her, time I get here to the time I leave." Doris, at whom this was directed, stuck out her tongue at him.

"Mr. Painter — can you read or write?"

"What kind of a question is that to ask?" replied Painter. "Again, down on a man because you've got learning and he doesn't. That — — Oldfield had a sight of learning, and where did it get *him?* Answer me that, Mr. Inspector!"

"All right," said Mallow. "I take it you can't."

"Take it, then, and if I wasn't a poor old man with a gammy leg you'd be taking my boot up your backside with it."

Mallow disconcerted the old man by laughing. "No doubt," he said. "And I daresay I wouldn't be the first to get it... That's an uncommonly fine stick you have there."

"Aye, so it is," said Painter, holding it up. Uncommonly fine it was: polished ebony, with a handle of silver in the shape of a reptilian head with large onyx eyes. "It was a Christmas present from my friend Merryweather."

"Merryweather?" asked Mallow, surprised at the name cropping up here.

"A good friend — that's all," said Painter. He took a long pull at his pint. *"He* understood," he muttered. "He said he'd see me righted."

"Oh? When did he say that?"

Painter did not answer. After a moment he began muttering again. *"Make me not sighted like the basilisk: I have looked on thousands, who have sped the better by my regard..."*

"I beg your pardon?"

"Merryweather said that when he gave me the stick... the head is a basilisk... turns people to stone... hehe... Oldfield's stone dead now..." Painter's muttering died away. His head drooped and he began to snore.

Mallow went back to the bar and introduced himself again, this time by name. Doris, at first inclined to be a little standoffish with a policeman, was tickled by the discovery that they had the same name; she decided they must be some sort of cousins and was willing to converse.

"So, Doris — what can you tell me about this Merryweather?" asked Mallow.

"Well, sir, he's a gentleman who comes into the pub now and then, starting in November it was. He said he's a commercial traveler — never said what line he was in — traveling between Fenchester and Chiltonbury. Very affable he is, too — always has a joke or a story or a bit of chaff."

"And it was here he became acquainted with your grandfather?"

"Yes. One night Granddad was going on about Mr. Oldfield worse than usual. Mr. Merryweather was very interested and went over and got the whole story. Since then they've been thick as thieves — you saw that stick Mr. Merryweather gave Granddad for Christmas. Mr. Merryweather has one just like it."

"Your grandfather said Mr. Merryweather promised to see him righted. Do you know when he said that?"

"I didn't hear anything like that, but then there's a lot more said here than I have time to listen to."

"I daresay. What does Mr. Merryweather look like?"

"Hmm — not young and not old. Middle-sized and stout — red hair and side-whiskers — old-fashioned spectacles. Old-fashioned in his dress, too — always wears a blue coat and a plaid vest."

"If he comes in again, please ask him to get in touch with me. Here's my card. Of course, he may do so on his own when he hears of the murder." *Or he may not.* "One more thing, Doris. Can you tell me where I can find your mother?"

"Oh, she'll be at home. Turn left after you go out the door, then left again, and you'll see our house. Painted white, it is, with a blue door and shutters."

"Thank you," replied Mallow. "Too early to go back to Swannington," he said to Bellman, "and not enough time to follow this Merryweather's trail to Chiltonbury. Let's knock off for lunch. We'll check on Painter's alibi afterwards. And since we're off duty, we can wash it down with — What would you recommend, Doris?"

"Oh, sir, nothing's so good as our Folly ale."

"Three pints of Folly ale with our lunch, then."

"We're beginning to get a line on this Merryweather," commented

Mallow over lunch. "We know what he looks like, we know what he does —"

"We know what he says he does," replied Bellman.

"Yes. We know Oldfield paid him a thousand pounds in December, and we know where he banks. What we don't know is whether he's our X."

"Sounds like a pretty distinctive person," suggested Henley. "Should be easy to find."

"Touch wood when you say things like that," said Mallow.

"Yes, sir," said Henley, grinning and rapping the table.

9

A FINE OLD ROW-DE-DOW

Before leaving Minstrel Folly they called on Betsey Mallow and found her at home. She was plump and black-eyed like Doris, but silver-haired. She also resembled her daughter in finding it a joke that her husband and Mallow had the same name, and in having little respect for Silas Painter.

"Of course I got out of that ratty old cottage and married Ted Mallow as soon as I could, leave or no leave," she told the inspector. "I'd have like to died of the rheumatics there, with the rain and the wind coming in all the time, and so would Dad, except he's too stubborn to die — all the Painters are like that."

"Was your father in his house Sunday night?" asked Mallow.

"Sure he was. I'd left him a bit of supper, and when I stopped by he'd eaten it, and I stayed and saw him safe in bed before I came home."

"Can you tell me when you got to your father's house, and when you left?"

"Of course. Dad's got a fine clock in that house, Mr. Oldfield saw to that. Not that *he'd* ever bother to wind it, I have to do it." Betsey

Mallow laughed. "If I didn't, he wouldn't know what time to go to the Wyvern!"

"Yes, but the times?"

"Oh, I was a little behindhand here, so I didn't get there until eight o'clock — and did I get a word of thanks for coming through all that snow? No, it was all 'You're late, a fine daughter you are leaving your poor old Dad all alone, you wouldn't care if I lived or died.' Not that I minded much, that's just his way. And it was just on nine when I left."

"That leaves Painter with not much of an alibi," remarked Bellman as they drove back to Swannington. "An hour's gap at each end."

"If he called on Oldfield, he didn't go to the front door —" began Mallow.

"Not him. He'd have gone to the back," said Bellman.

" — Or, as I was about to say, the back. Surely, though, if he had, one of the servants would have mentioned it."

"We didn't ask."

"We will. Could Oldfield have let him in through the French window?"

"And got up and locked it when Painter left after killing him?"

"Good point. He's illiterate, too — did the note mean justice, though moving slowly, had finally caught up with the man who'd turned him off his land? I shouldn't have thought he had any poetry in him."

"What about those words he said about a — what was it, a basilisk?" put in Henley. "Those were pretty poetic."

"He got them from Merryweather," said Mallow. "They sound like a quotation. I shall have to look it up."

"Shakespeare," said Bellman. *"The Winter's Tale."*

Constable Pyke had not finished going through the bank records. Mallow detailed Henley to assist him while he and Bellman visited

Oldfield's shop. The shop was on the outskirts of the south side of Swannington, well away from the High Road. It was wholly unsuited to the town, being in the same brutally functional style as the workshop at Minstrel Manor. Two large doors faced on to the street; Mallow presumed they were for lorries to deliver or carry off machinery and materials. On one side was a smaller door which led into the offices. Mallow rang the bell and was admitted by Bob Attkinson, who had been expecting him, and was taken to Attkinson's office. The manager, a square-built, square-headed man in his fifties, sat down behind a desk cluttered with papers and bits of metal. A large steel bolt served as a paperweight.

"I'll do anything I can to help you, Inspector," said Attkinson, taking up a pipe and looking into the bowl.

"Thank you, Mr. Attkinson," replied Mallow. "To begin with, how long have you managed the shop?"

"Since it was first set up," said Attkinson, setting down the pipe and taking a tobacco pouch from a pocket.

"That was in 1915?"

"Yes." He filled the bowl of the pipe and tamped down the tobacco.

"How did you come to be the manager here?"

"Recommended to Mr. Oldfield. Where did I put those matches?" The manager began rooting about in the papers on his desk.

Bellman gave him a box.

"By whom?"

"Booth & Bixby." Attkinson struck a match and made a business of lighting his pipe.

"And who are they?"

"Firm I worked for before coming here." The match had not done its job well enough; Attkinson struck another.

"What do they do?"

"Not in business any more."

"What *did* they do?"

"Machinery."

"Making, repairing, or transporting?"

"Making," The pipe had gone out. Attkinson struck another match.

"What sort of machinery."

"Lathes, drills, jigsaws, that sort of thing."

"What was your impression of Mr. Oldfield?"

"Can't say much."

"Why not?"

"Only met him a few times."

"Who gave you instructions, then?"

"Mr. Cabell."

"What is your impression of Mr. Cabell?"

"Knows his stuff."

"Do you know of any employee or former employee who might have a grudge against Mr. Oldfield?"

Attkinson puffed on his pipe and looked out the window. After a minute he said, "Can't think of one at the moment."

"Do you have records of the men who have worked here?"

Attkinson took his pipe from his mouth and peered into the bowl. Having apparently decided it wasn't working fast enough, he lit another match and applied it to the smoldering tobacco. Mallow fought back an impulse to pick up the bolt and reconstruct Oldfield's murder. "Yes," the manager finally said.

"One of my men will come here to look through them."

"Mm-hmm," grunted Attkinson.

Mallow took the grunt as assent. "Is there anyone else here I can speak to?" he asked.

"Yes."

"Where can I find him?"

"In back."

"Thank you."

Outside of Attkinson's office, Mallow said, "Did you get all that down, Bellman?"

"Yes, sir," replied Bellman with a straight face.

In the back they found a small, bird-like man working alone. He gave his name as Harry Bledsoe, and proved to be much more conversable than Attkinson, to Mallow's relief.

"You don't want to mind Bob Attkinson," he said, as if reading Mallow's mind. "He's good at his job and you can't say fairer than that — always gets the right man for a job, never a hitch when something's needed, never missed a schedule in twelve years, not even when we had six projects going on at the same time and men coming and going round the clock on each of 'em — but doesn't have a thought in his head outside of it, and won't use two words when one will do."

"The shop doesn't look too busy at the moment," observed Mallow.

"Well, it comes and goes, like. Right now there's just the solar lamp we're working on and that's mostly electrical. You see, we don't have a permanent staff — just Bob to manage the shop and me because whatever's going on they'll need electricity to run the equipment. If something comes in that wants machining, or carpentry, or chemicals — there's plenty of workmen out of a job, or could still use a little extra, so Bob goes and finds 'em and takes 'em on till that bit of work is done."

"I see. About Mr. Oldfield — what was your impression of him?"

"Hard to say, and that's a fact. He never came around much, and never said much when he came. I suppose he was shy around people, for all he was so clever."

"Was there ever any trouble with any of the workmen?" asked Mallow.

"One or two, maybe, early on," replied Bledsoe. "But Bob made it clear as crystal he wouldn't stand for it. Once word got around that any man who crossed the line — don't get me wrong, Bob can make allowances for human nature and nobody ever felt he had to hold his breath and walk on tiptoe — but any man who crossed the line was out the door for good — well, there wasn't any trouble after that."

"Can you remember any incidents?"

"None recently, I can tell you that. Let me think for a minute."

"Oh, Inspector?" called Attkinson, coming into the shop. "I do remember one employee."

"Yes?" replied Mallow.

"His name was Thomas Hackett." In a burst of loquacity, the manager went on unprompted. "He was sacked in 1920."

"Oh, Lord, I'd forgot him!" said Bledsoe. "Don't know how I came to do that — it was a nine-days' wonder around here."

"Tell me about it, please," said Mallow. *Hackett? Could it be?*

"Well, Tom Hackett was a machinist, and a good one — give him a plan and a few scraps and he'd turn you out anything from a pair of scissors to an aeroplane. Mind you, he needed a plan — he couldn't *invent* anything, not like Mr. Oldfield could. But what he could do, now and then, was improve. He'd learned a lot about this and that, so he'd be building something, smooth as you please, and he'd get an idea how to change the design to make it faster or more powerful, or do something besides what it was supposed to; or he'd combine it with something totally different we were working on. He'd run to Bob with it and Bob would have to sit on him and tell him to stick to the plan." Bledsoe suddenly guffawed. "There was the radio-furnace — Hackett had this cock-eyed idea it could be used for cooking. He'd bring his lunch from home and use our working model to heat it up. Remember that time the steak-and-kidney pie exploded, Bob? But sometimes Bob would call Mr. Cabell and tell him Hackett was on to something, and then he and Mr. Oldfield would come to the shop and sit down with Hackett and listen to his idea — and they let him go ahead."

"So what happened?"

"Well, like Bob said, this was in 1920. We had a lot going on then — besides the radio-furnace there was the climate-controller, and, let me see, the automatic telephone message-taker — a shame, we never did get that one to work — and we were just finishing up the timer-switch —"

"And the railway speedometer," put in Attkinson.

"Right. Anyhow, Hackett was working on some of them and got

one of his ideas. Mr. Oldfield and Mr. Cabell were visiting that day and Hackett decided he'd go straight to Mr. Oldfield with it. So he found Mr. Oldfield and took him over to his workbench to show him. The next thing you know, Hackett's shouting at Mr. Oldfield and Mr. Oldfield's shouting at Hackett. Bob and Mr. Cabell come running from Bob's office and there's a fine old row-de-dow; and the end of the story is, Bob told Hackett to go home and not come back."

"And that was that?"

"Yes. It was a bloody — 'scuse me — a ruddy shame he and his missus died right after."

"Died?"

"Burned to death in their house," said Bledsoe, shaking his head. "I heard his girl wasn't there, though, the Lord be praised. She went away — to London, I think. I never heard what happened to her. Hackett used to bring her to work with him sometimes, till Bob put a stop to it. She was always wandering around, poking into things and asking questions. Didn't bother me, but drove some of the other men batty."

"Her name wouldn't have been Edwina, would it?"

"That's it," said Bledsoe. "Edwina."

"I've met her. She's alive and, I understand, doing quite well." *And hasn't changed a bit.*

Collecting Pyke and Henley, Mallow returned to Fenchester. At headquarters he found Porlock waiting for him. "I couldn't —" he began.

Mallow gestured to him to wait. "Ring up Minstrel Manor and ask for Mr. Cabell," he said, addressing Sergeant Spenser, who was on duty, "and put the call through to my office." Porlock followed him there and stood patiently.

Mallow's telephone rang and he picked up the receiver. "Mr. Cabell?"

"Yes, Inspector. What do you want? Please keep it short — I must get back to my work."

"Can you tell me how you came to employ Pembert?"

"So you've tracked down the criminal mastermind?" replied Cabell, amusement in his voice. "Poor Pembert. I assure you, Inspector, he's no Moriarty."

"I'm not interested in his degree of villainy, Mr. Cabell. That is on record. I'm asking you to confirm his account of himself."

"You may rely upon it, Inspector."

"In your own words, please?"

Cabell sighed. "When we purchased Minstrel Manor, Pembert came to us from Howard Draven. I believe I told you this already. He made no secret of his past: he had been convicted of forgery, and had just been released from prison. Draven vouched for him, even though he had been the victim of Pembert's crime. He also referred us to the prison authorities, who told us Pembert's — I should say, Pemberton's — conduct had been exemplary and they were confident of his rehabilitation. The man has done an entirely satisfactory job as a butler here for the past six years."

"Thank you. One other question. What do you know of a man called Barnabas Merryweather?"

"Very little. Mr. Oldfield had some dealings with him, but I was not privy to them."

"Did you ever meet him?"

"No. Is that all?"

"Could —" There was a click as Cabell hung up. "Blast," said Mallow. He called Spenser and told him to ring up the manor again and ask for Miss Hackett. "Now, what is it, Porlock?"

"I couldn't get a copy of the *Panopticon,* sir," reported Porlock. "The last newsagent I visited called the magazine's offices in London while I was there and ordered one. They'll put it in the post and it should arrive tomorrow."

"Good enough." His telephone rang again and he picked it up. "Miss Hackett?"

"No, sir," came Spenser's voice. "Miss Hackett is not at the manor. They don't know when she'll return."

"Damn her," said Mallow, hanging up. "I told her to stay there… Get Bellman, Henley, and Pyke in here and we'll have another conference."

"So what did you find at the bank?" asked Mallow when the others had arrived. "Any more cheques to Merryweather?"

"Six in all," replied Pyke. "The first was in September of last year, the last in December. Each one was for a thousand pounds."

"Six thousand pounds in four months? And he was keeping them from Cabell? What were he and Merryweather up to?"

"Gambling debts?" suggested Porlock.

"Dope?" put in Henley.

"Blackmail?" contributed Pyke.

"Not dope," said Bellman. "If he'd been doping, it would have come out in the post-mortem. And not blackmail, either. Blackmailers take cash. A cheque is as good as a signed confession."

"How would Oldfield get the cash?" argued Pyke. "He hardly ever left the manor. And if he were being blackmailed, the last thing he'd do would be to ask Cabell or Pembert to get it for him. The blackmailer could be using 'Merryweather' as an alias. As soon as Oldfield was finished paying up, he'd disappear."

"But it's still risky," replied Bellman. "At any time Oldfield could decide exposure was better than paying up, and inform the police. We'd freeze or attach Merryweather's account. Not only would he have to bolt without the money, it would be evidence against him."

"Only if he's leaving the money in the account. We don't know if he's depositing the cheques, or cashing them."

"We'll find that out when we visit the bank tomorrow," said Mallow. "Meanwhile, you're forgetting the papers we found in the study. Someone had been forging Oldfield's name, or preparing to."

"Forgery implies embezzlement," said Porlock. "And the most likely embezzler is Cabell. He knew of Pembert's past. Say Cabell and Pembert, working together —"

"Not Cabell," interrupted Pyke. "He had the handling of Oldfield's affairs. There must be a dozen more subtle ways by which he could embezzle than writing huge cheques to a non-existent person with a bizarre name. Pembert alone, now — there's a possibility. He'd done it once already."

"And was caught out at once," said Bellman. "*Maybe* he'd try again. I can see him forging one cheque and doing a bunk with the cash. But six, over several months? He'd be begging to be sent back to prison."

"Pembert and Muirdyke, then," said Porlock.

"Aren't we forgetting something?" asked Henley. "Whoever was forging Oldfield's name was forging Merryweather's also. How does *that* fit in with embezzlement, *or* blackmail?"

"We don't *know* the same person was forging both names," replied Pyke. "They were on separate sheets of paper."

"Are you asking us to believe in two different forgers?" objected Henley. "Really, Pyke, you must learn to control —"

Mallow held up his hand. "Gentlemen, we're getting ahead of ourselves again. Let's find Merryweather. A little third-degree — all right, Bellman, I'm only joking — and he'll come across."

"What about Thomas Hackett?" asked Bellman.

"We know it wasn't him," replied Mallow. Pyke opened his mouth to speak but Mallow forestalled him. "No, Pyke. I refuse to believe that Thomas Hackett faked his own death and waited seven years to take revenge. And I can't see Miss Hackett murdering Oldfield because her father had been sacked seven years earlier."

"Motives can be improbable, sir," said Pyke. "You said that yourself."

"So I did. Some are more improbable than others. Still, we'll talk to her. Meanwhile, Henley, tomorrow you and Vanderleun can start looking for Merryweather here in Fenchester. Pyke and Porlock can assist you."

"Why here?" asked Henley.

"He told Doris he was a commercial traveler, going between Fenchester and Chiltonbury. It may or may not have been a taradiddle. Unfortunately, he didn't say what he traveled in. Try the principal shops — yes, and the wholesalers too. He may have stayed overnight on his visits, so try the hotels as well."

"What if he lives in Fenchester and visits Chiltonbury?"

"If he has a place of his own, he'll be in the town records; but we may wind up asking at lodging houses. I'll ask the Superintendent to ring up Carstairs in Chiltonbury and arrange a search there. We'll have to inform him anyway that we'll be in his bailiwick, asking questions at Merryweather's bank. Spenser can ring up the bank and arrange a time. And, while I think of it, I'll have him get in touch with Scotland Yard and ask if they know Merryweather's name. Damn, it's getting late and I still have my report to write."

Mallow was near the end of his report when Pyke knocked and entered.

"What is it, Pyke?"

"I was going through the records from Oldfield's workshop at the manor — the cheques and the ledgers."

"Yes?"

"The payments to Merryweather aren't there."

"Indeed? Cabell said he didn't know what Oldfield and Merryweather were up to, but I'm surprised he didn't even know about the payments. Six thousand pounds is a lot of money. I'll have to press him on that. Thank you, Pyke."

Pyke did not leave at once. "Sir?"

"What else?"

"It occurred to me there might be records in Mr. Oldfield's safe."

"But Cabell said he didn't use it — of course, that's as far as *Cabell* knew. And only Oldfield had the combination. Wait a moment." Mallow picked up his telephone and asked Spenser to ring up the shop in Swannington. "I hope Attkinson or Bledsoe is still there... Hullo — is that Mr. Bledsoe? This is Inspector Mallow. Do you remember if Mr. Oldfield's book-safe was one of the things you worked on? It was? Would you be able to open one? You wouldn't? Thanks, and sorry to have troubled you." He hung up. "So much for that idea. We'll have to ask the Yard for an expert. I'll put it to the Superintendent when I hand in my report. Good thinking, Pyke."

"Thank you, sir."

10

MISS HACKETT AND I ARE OLD FRIENDS

Edwina spent most of Wednesday morning after breakfast trying to work on Oldfield's portrait and not getting very far. At eleven she decided to go for a drive to clear her head. Passing through the hall she was accosted by Cabell. "Miss Hackett!" he said. "May I ask a favour? My car is still in Fenchester — at the railway station —"

"And you need someone to drive you in to fetch it?"

"Yes. Ordinarily I would have taken our own car and had Pembert drive, but he is indisposed this morning —"

"I'm not surprised, after the dreadful shock he had — Mr. Oldfield being murdered —"

"— and William is a menace on the road. If you would be so kind?"

"I'd be happy to. I've been trying to get back into finishing the portrait and I can't. In fact, I was just going out."

As Edwina's battered two-seater was turning on to the High Road, a black car passed them going the other way. "Hullo," she said. "That was the inspector. And the Sergeant — I forget his name."

"Are you sure?" asked Cabell. "I only caught a glimpse."

"Oh, yes. I'm good with faces. Should we go back? He may want to talk to us."

"He can wait. I want my car back. There are modifications to it that haven't been patented yet."

"What sort of modifications? Or are they a secret?"

"An improved carburettor, for one thing. And special tyres for driving in snow. This is an Abbey we're riding in, isn't it?"

"Yes. Are you interested in cars?"

"Anything mechanical. I've never seen an Abbey before. Aren't they expensive?"

"This one wasn't. I bought it second-hand. Maybe third or fourth, considering the shape it's in. I'd like to swap it for something newer. What do you drive?"

"An Albert, although, as I said, it's been modified." Cabell went on talking about his car. Edwina, who was not mechanically minded, let his words flow over her, catching only "rear-wheel drive," "four-cylinder engine," and "aluminium body," until he stopped and said, "I'm afraid I've been boring you."

"Oh, not at all," replied Edwina — truthfully, as she had been occupied with her own thoughts. "What will happen to Mr. Oldfield's work now that he's gone?"

"Oh, I'll keep on with it and finish up what he started. That is, as best I can without him. There is plenty to work on — for every idea completed he had two new ones."

"Do you think the *Panopticon* will still want his portrait?"

"I have no idea. The magazine may cancel the article — or at least postpone it."

"I *hope* they don't cancel it," exclaimed Edwina with feeling. "I was counting on it."

Conversation stopped while she slowed and carefully maneuvered around a lorry with a flat tyre. Once past, Cabell spoke. "If the loss of the commission will cause you hardship, I'd be happy to buy the painting myself."

"That's very kind of you. It's not so much the money; I have a job waiting for me in Rutlandshire, so I shan't starve or be turned out into the snow. It's just that it *was* rather a big thing for me — getting my name out there and all that."

"Will you be remaining at the manor?" he asked. "I suppose, though, you would wish to leave. Mr. Oldfield's — demise — must be very distressing to you."

"Not at all," she replied. "Oh — that came out wrong. I'm very sorry about Mr. Oldfield. I didn't get to know him very well, but I should have liked to. He struck me as a good man."

"But that he was murdered — that doesn't disturb you?"

"No. Does that disturb *you?*"

"Not at all. The ability to face up to unpleasantness is an admirable trait. I wish it were more common. People who hide from their problems cause so much trouble, and not only for themselves. Especially about money —" He stopped.

"You mean Mr. Muirdyke? He doesn't seem to *hide* from his problems."

"No, he doesn't. You are correct — Muirdyke is a bad example of what I'm talking about. But even so, he was a grief to his uncle."

"And yet they seem to have been fond of each other."

"Yes. I believe they were."

They were now passing through Swannington. Edwina stopped to allow an elderly woman to cross the road. As they started to move on she looked back and exclaimed, "Good heavens, that was Mrs. Gilpin. I used to go to her sweetshop when I was a girl."

"You grew up in Swannington, then?" asked Cabell.

"No. I was born in London and we lived there until I was eleven. Then we moved to Fenshire. We lived in a little house in Ranulf's Crossing. Dad's job was in Swannington and sometimes he brought me to the machine shop where he worked. I'm afraid sometimes I was a bother to the other men working there. One of them used to give me sixpences to go away —" She broke off, staring at Cabell. "It was you!"

"I?" said Cabell, surprised.

"Yes. You were younger then, of course, and not so thin, but I remember your face. Maybe you don't remember me but you must remember Dad — Thomas Hackett?"

"Of course! So you're Hackett's little girl — that's a strange coincidence... What is he doing now?"

"He's dead. He and my mother died when our house burned down."

"Oh, I'm sorry to hear that. When did it happen?"

"Some time ago — when I was sixteen. Funny how memories come back," Edwina mused. "I was going to visit my aunt — I remember I was packing — Dad came home in a frightful wax. I'd never known him to be so angry. He stormed up and down, calling — yes, it *was* Oldfield — every name in the book. One thing sticks in my head: he said Oldfield wouldn't know a hawk from a handsaw no matter where the wind was blowing from. What was it all about?"

"I remember he quarreled with Mr. Oldfield, but not the details," said Cabell. "Mr. Oldfield had to let Hackett go."

"I'm glad this didn't come out while I was painting him. It could have made things a little awkward."

"Perhaps not. The next day Mr. Oldfield had cooled down. He sent your father a letter of recommendation and a cheque for — yes, for £250."

"The next thing I remember is my aunt breaking the news to me... The cheque probably burned up with everything else. If not — if Dad had managed to put the money in the bank before he died — then Mr. Oldfield helped pay for me to learn to paint his portrait."

"It's a strange world."

"Getting back to the portrait — I ought to finish it, anyway, so I'll be staying on for that. Or not. I can do it at home."

"Can you finish the portrait without Mr. Oldfield?"

"Oh, yes. Most of what remains to be done is background. And, as I said, I have a very good memory for faces... I suppose it's awful cheek asking, but may I stay on after it's done? I do want to follow the investigation."

"I wouldn't mind," replied Cabell, smiling. "But I suppose it's really up to Mr. Muirdyke. The manor is his now."

"I'll need an excuse..." Edwina thought for a minute. "Got it. Kympole — that's where I live — is just a few miles past Fenchester. I'll go on to there, get some proper materials, and do sketches of the people at the manor. Would you mind sitting for yours?"

"Of course not. I'm very busy, but — let me think — perhaps tomorrow after lunch?"

"That will do."

Edwina dropped off Cabell at the railway station and motored on to Kympole and her small cottage. She stayed just long enough to pick up a pad of sketching paper and an assortment of charcoal pencils. Realising she was hungry, she looked into her larder and found it empty.

At the newsagent-cum-post office she picked up her accumulated mail and a copy of the Fenchester *Times* before going on to the Earl of Fenshire for a quick lunch.

Passing under the pub's curious sign displaying a robed and coroneted mouse, Edwina went in, asked for bread and cheese and a lemon squash, and settled down at a table. A couple of acquaintances waved greetings to her but didn't come over, from which she gathered Oldfield's murder, or at least her own connection with it, had not become common knowledge. After going through her mail — three bills, two circulars, and a letter — she scanned the newspaper. There was a report of the crime: it was not as prominent as she had feared and suggested Oldfield had met his death at the hands of a burglar. Her name was not mentioned. *That's a relief — there are some kinds of publicity I* don't *need.* She noted with interest the statement from Superintendent Runciman that although this was Mallow's first murder case, "it's a good start for a bright and zealous young inspector and I have perfect confidence he'll bring the culprit to

justice." *His first murder case, and he's had to put up with me being imperti-*
nent to him all over the place. I must learn to behave better... She put down
the paper and opened the letter; it proved to be from Dorothy
Mowbray, a friend from her time at art school.

The furnishings of the hall at Minstrel Manor included a writing desk
stocked with paper, pens, ink, envelopes, and stamps. Upon her
return, Edwina sat down at the desk and wrote a reply to the letter
from Dorothy.

Dear Dot,

*SO happy to hear your news. Rodney certainly took his time before
popping the question, didn't he? I was beginning to think the Major had
changed his mind about letting his son and heir tie himself up to a nobody
that messes about with paints. All right, you're not* really *a nobody, but how
far does being the first cousin (once removed) to an Earl get you? My great-
grandfather was manager of the stables at Hampton Court, but do I get
invites to Buckingham Palace?*

*Will you go on painting after you're married? It always seemed to me you
took it up only because you had nothing going on in your life and it was a
way to pass the time. Well, if you give it up that's O.K. by me — means less
competition for us REAL artists.*

*Have I got something to tell YOU! I was invited to a real live Manor (see
the posh letterhead?) to paint the owner, a dear old boy called Sebastian
Oldfield. Well, a couple of days ago the dear old boy got himself
MURDERED! Honest to God — there's been a Detective-Inspector here,
detecting and inspecting like anything.*

*It happened in Mr. Oldfield's study. The funny thing is, I was next door
in the library and didn't hear a thing. I wish I had — then I could do
something to help. I liked Mr. Oldfield, and I like the Inspector — but I don't
think he likes me. Partly because I snooped around the study before he*

arrived. Yes, with the body there and everything — you used to tell me I had enough curiosity to kill a dozen cats. Unfortunately, I didn't find any clues (that I know of).

Apart from the servants, the only other people here are John Cabell, Mr. Oldfield's assistant, and his nephew, Charles Muirdyke. Mr. Cabell strikes me as an odd fish, very remote, until you get him on the subject of motorcars, but I think he's human underneath. Mr. Muirdyke is much more transparent: lazy, irresponsible — but basically sound, and will do well if he grows up.

I suppose I ought to be worried, possibly being in the same house as a murderer — but I can't believe it was anyone here. I know in the stories the murderer carries on afterwards perfectly normally, but real life can't be like that. I'm sure if I ever killed anyone I'd be a complete nervous wreck.

Anyhow, I'm hoping the murder is cleared up before I have to leave. I think I can wangle an invite to stay on — we'll see.

Books go so much faster — crime in first chapter, solution in last chapter, and one gets from one to the other in one or two hours. Here it's been almost two days and it feels like it's been two weeks.

Hope my next will be the last chapter. My love to you and Rodney. Let me know when you've set a date.

Congratulations again,

Edie

P.S. Try and get Rodney away from the Bright Young People before he winds up dead, disinherited, or in a nursing home. E.

Edwina was putting her letter into an envelope when Muirdyke's voice came from behind her. "Hullo, Miss Hackett," he greeted her. "I'm just back from the Wyvern."

"How's our friend Painter?"

"Him? He wasn't there... I say — do you think you could dine with me tonight?"

"Oh!" said Edwina. It took her a moment to collect her thoughts. "I'd — I'd like to, but I haven't got anything suitable to wear. If I'd known, I'd have picked up my evening dress when I went home for my sketching gear."

"Don't worry about that," Muirdyke reassured her. "We only dressed for dinner when Uncle Sebastian had to entertain someone important in the way of business, like a company director or an M.P. Come to think of it, that's the only time we dined together at all. Uncle Sebastian always ate in his study and Cabell usually in the workshop."

"And you?"

"Me? I wander into the kitchen and scrounge whenever I'm hungry. But what do you say?"

"Very well. It will be a change from a tray in the library."

"I'll tell Pembert. Cocktails in the drawing room at 5:30?"

"All right."

Edwina entered the drawing room promptly at 5:30. Muirdyke was already there. He came forward, smiling, to greet her. "I say —" he began, but stopped short when Cabell entered, clad in full evening regalia of white tie and boiled shirt. His smile vanished. A moment later Pembert came in with the cocktail tray. Muirdyke muttered an excuse and followed the butler out.

"What's Cabell doing here?" he asked. "I didn't invite *him.*"

"I'm very sorry, Mr. Charles," replied Pembert. "You told me you were dining tonight, but not that it was to be just you and Miss Hackett. Encountering Mr. Cabell, I thought it proper to inform him."

"Oh, very well," grumbled Muirdyke. "I wish he hadn't shown up in the soup-and-fish. It's dashed awkward for me and Miss Hackett, though. I don't know what to do." He turned to go back into the drawing room and met Cabell coming out.

"After seeing Miss Hackett in mufti, I thought I'd change into something less formal," said Cabell. "I shan't be long."

"Ah," replied Muirdyke. At the door of the drawing room he turned and called after Cabell, "Take your time."

"I'm glad to find Pembert's better," said Edwina when Muirdyke returned.

"Eh?"

"I heard from Mr. Cabell earlier today he was ill."

"Why didn't — oh. I suppose they're used to going to Cabell when my uncle isn't around."

"But now you're lord of the manor. So what are you going to do?"

"I haven't the faintest idea," replied Muirdyke. "I don't know beans about running an estate and even less about Uncle Sebastian's work. I shall have to keep Cabell on. I don't particularly like the fellah, but he knows what's what."

"What will you do about Todd and Hallam?" Edwina took a sip of her gin-and-tonic, grimaced, and put it down. "This is awfully strong. I'd better not have any more if I'm going to drink wine with dinner."

"Todd and Hallam? Ring them up and tell them I'm resigning. That will be something new — a change from getting the boot at any rate… On second thoughts I'd better not. I'll just tell them my uncle died suddenly, I'm his only relative, and I'll be tied up for a few days dealing with this and that."

"Why not resign?"

"Uncle Sebastian may have changed his will. The last time I was here he cut up a little rougher than usual about some money I dropped on the nags." Abruptly he changed the subject. "How's his portrait coming along?"

"I should have it finished in a day or so."

"I say, would you mind staying on afterwards for a bit?"

Edwina laughed. "I was going to ask if I may. I'd like to do some sketch portraits of the people here — oh, I might as well admit it, that's just an excuse. I really want to see how the investigation turns out."

Cabell returned, now wearing a suit as tweedy as Muirdyke's. As he came through the door, three melodic chimes echoed in the air. Edwina looked about but could not see the source.

"Time to go in to dinner," said Cabell, seeing Edwina's bewilderment. "Mr. Oldfield's touch again. He said anyone could have a dinner gong." Muirdyke approached Edwina to take her to dinner but Cabell got in ahead of him. "I claim the privilege," he said. "Miss Hackett and I are old friends."

11

DINNER AND A HARD-BOILED EGG

"What do you mean, 'old friends?'" said Muirdyke to Cabell when they were seated around the dinner table.

It was Edwina who replied. "Dad used to work for Mr. Oldfield," she said. "He took me to the workshop now and then. I must have been a bother because Mr. Cabell would pay me to go away."

"You didn't tell me that yesterday."

"I only recognised Mr. Cabell this morning while driving him in to Fenchester. I never met Mr. Oldfield at the shop. If I had, I'd have known him the moment I started on the portrait."

"You remember faces that well, then?"

"Oh, yes. Here, I'll show you." Edwina fished in a pocket of her skirt and came up with a small pad and a pencil stub. Rapidly she drew the faces of Mallow, Bellman, and Pyke. "Of course, these may not count — I met them only yesterday. This will convince Mr. Cabell at any rate." She added Bob Attkinson and Harry Bledsoe to the collection.

"Amazing," said Cabell. "That's them — as they were seven years ago."

The discussion was interrupted by Pembert and William serving soup. As soon as it was on the table, Edwina said, "I'm sure we all have the same question on our minds: who did it?"

"Did what?" asked Cabell.

"Killed Mr. Oldfield."

Cabell frowned. "Isn't it a little unseemly for us to sit here at Mr. Oldfield's table, less than two days after he was murdered, and casually speculate about who might have killed him?"

"Certainly not," replied Muirdyke. "If the police can do it, why can't we? Surely we — at least you and I — have as much interest as they in finding out who did it. Maybe more. Dash it all, I *liked* the old boy."

"So did I," put in Edwina. "Even though I didn't get to know him very well."

Cabell shrugged and said, "Well, then, I knew him better than either of you and liked him quite as much. And, I suppose, if it had happened the other way round — if he were here and I'd been killed — he wouldn't have objected to talking about it. Quite the reverse, in fact."

"There you are, then," said Muirdyke. "If you ask me, it's dashed strange. I don't see why he should get himself murdered at all. I mean, anybody would have said he hadn't an enemy in the world."

"Of course, he may not have been murdered out of enmity," said Edwina. "He might have known something, or been in someone's way. The inspector thinks it was likely a burglar."

"How do you know that?" asked Muirdyke.

"It was in today's Fenchester *Times*."

"I was responsible for that," said Cabell. "I thought it best to forestall publicity, so I rang up the *Times* yesterday as soon as the inspector left and gave them the burglar story. They won't be very interested in anything as mundane as that."

"But you don't think it was one?" asked Muirdyke.

"No."

"Then let's get on with it," said Edwina.

"One must be analytic about it," said Cabell. "Who are our

suspects? But before proceeding, shall we agree we cannot exclude any of us? One of the three people at this table could be a murderer."

"I insist on ruling out Miss Hackett," said Muirdyke.

"I concur. One of us two, then —"

Edwina interrupted. "I refuse to be ruled out. The suspects are everyone who —" She stopped as Pembert and William came in with the next course. When they were gone, she resumed. "Everyone who was near the study between seven and ten. William was there at seven, Pembert at ten; and I was in the library the entire time."

"We shan't get far *that* way," objected Muirdyke. "William? He can't stand the sight of blood. Pembert? He hasn't a violent bone in his body — and he was devoted to Uncle Sebastian."

"The butler *didn't* do it," said Edwina.

"Exactly."

"Then I must be the murderer."

"Tosh!" said Muirdyke.

"Your logic is incomplete, Miss Hackett," said Cabell. "At any time the murderer could have come along the passage, or through the French window, or down the stair from Mr. Oldfield's room."

"None of those is possible," said Edwina. "If he came along the passage, I should have seen him. The French window was locked. If it was the stairway, it must have been one of the servants — but I'm in agreement with Mr. Muirdyke it couldn't have been either Pembert or William, and the rest of the servants alibi each other."

"How do you know that?" asked Cabell.

"I overheard the sergeant — I forget his name — telling the inspector."

"And the locked window?"

"I went into the study and looked about before the constable arrived."

"You went in — with Uncle Sebastian there dead and all?" said Muirdyke.

"I'm afraid I did." Cabell raised one eyebrow as if trying to fathom the enormity of her behaviour. Muirdyke whistled. Edwina thought it sounded more admiring than shocked.

"Did you see any clues?" asked Cabell.

"No," confessed Edwina. "I saw he'd finished dining, but that isn't a clue. So it comes back to me. Or does it?"

"It does not. We agreed we could not rule out anyone at this table. Let us consider Muirdyke."

"Why me?" asked Muirdyke.

"It's quite simple," replied Cabell. "You had a motive for killing your uncle. He made no secret of the contents of his will: you inherit the manor and a considerable amount of money. The question before us now is this: do you have an alibi?"

"Of course I do! I was at the Wyvern all evening!"

"And were you in the company of one or more persons the entire time?"

"Well — some of it." Muirdyke repeated the account he had given Inspector Mallow the day before.

"There — you see?" said Cabell. "Time enough to go, commit the crime, and return."

"What about you?" retorted Muirdyke. "You had the same motive as I. Where's *your* alibi?"

"I wasn't here," said Cabell, unruffled. "I had left at seven to drive to Fenchester… I suppose, then," he added with a smile, "as the only one of the suspects *with* an alibi, I'm the obvious candidate for the murderer."

Conversation flagged for a time. Cabell sat musing, occasionally sipping his glass of water. Edwina watched him, his thin intellectual face immobile in the flickering candlelight. From time to time she glanced at Muirdyke, who was drinking Cabell's share of the wine as well as his own.

"Well then," she said. "We've established we're all possibly guilty. Why not spread the net wider? The murderer could have come from outside the house — which is what I think really happened."

"Painter!" exclaimed Muirdyke. "It must have been Painter! You heard what he said about Uncle Sebastian."

"Who is Painter?" asked Cabell.

"You should know," said Muirdyke. "Uncle Sebastian took his farm away from him to carry out some sort of experiments. I'm surprised at that — for all he loved melodrama, he never struck me as the hard-hearted landlord turning his tenant out into the snow."

"Oh, him. I'd forgot about him. Your uncle had a perfect right to do what he did. The Painters had been tenants of Minstrel Manor for generations. The lease had been granted originally to Silas Painter's great-grandfather on a three-lives basis, meaning it was held by that Painter, his son, and his grandson — who was Silas Painter's father — and expired on the grandson's death. This occurred many years ago, when Sir Cholmondeley Maunder still owned the manor. Neither Sir Cholmondeley nor Silas Painter took any steps to renew the lease."

"Why didn't my uncle do something when he bought the manor? Or didn't he know?"

"He knew. We went into all these matters at the time. Mr. Oldfield saw no reason to bother; Painter was an old man, with no son, and a daughter married and living elsewhere. Later, when we wanted the farm, we consulted Mr. Oldfield's solicitor. He assured us Painter had no legal right to the farm — in his opinion, Painter had no moral right to it either, as he neglected it shamefully. Mr. Oldfield behaved quite generously. He would have been within his rights simply to have turned Painter out and left him to shift for himself; instead, he repaired and refurnished a house in Minstrel Folly where Painter lives, rent-free. He also set aside a certain amount of capital, which our bank holds in trust, that gives Painter a small income."

"Incidentally, what *was* Mr. Oldfield doing?" asked Edwina. "Painter thinks he was poisoning the soil."

"Your uncle was trying to find a chemical compound which would kill weeds but not crops. Painter's farm was a perfect testing ground — it was overrun with weeds."

"Something that kills weeds?" said Edwina. "I could use that. I have a little garden at my cottage — that is, I'm trying to have a little garden, but it gets choked every year without fail. Can you spare some?"

"Certainly," replied Cabell. "If I had any. We had little success. If anything, we kill the crops faster than the weeds. I've thought of taking it to the War Office."

"What for?"

"For use against the agricultural resources of an enemy — no food, no army. Our blockade of Germany during the Great War contributed a great deal to our victory."

"And to starving innocent women and children," retorted Edwina. "My brother was in Germany after the war —"

"I didn't know you had a brother," put in Muirdyke.

"I don't, any more. The Spanish flu got him. But the things he saw and heard — why, it's worse than gas."

"I agree with Miss Hackett," said Muirdyke. "Dashed unsporting."

"War isn't a sport," said Cabell. "But we're wandering from the point, aren't we? We were talking about Painter."

"Right," said Muirdyke. "He got some garbled idea of what Uncle Sebastian was doing. He got into the study and killed him."

"How?" asked Cabell.

"Through the window!"

"But I just said the window was locked," objected Edwina.

"Wait a minute!" cried Muirdyke. "I was reading a book the other day — *Murderers, Limited* — a gang of crooks had set up a murder business — you could order any kind of murder you liked — dashed interesting, actually —"

"Can we get to the point?" asked Cabell.

"Right-ho. Anyway, in the book somebody was hit on the head and got up and locked the door before he died!"

"I can still think of a few objections," said Edwina. "Why would your uncle have let him in? And supposing he had, surely Mr. Oldfield would have been on his guard. I saw the murder scene: there was no struggle. Your uncle was sitting at his desk when he was killed. It's a wide desk — Painter isn't tall enough to have reached across it to hit him, and he wouldn't have sat still while Painter picked up the paperweight and walked around the desk."

"I suppose you're — wait a minute!" said Muirdyke. "He could have swung that stick of his across the desk. You saw it — it had a heavy metal handle!"

"But the paperweight was bloodstained."

"He faked that afterwards."

"Would he have had the brains to do that?" asked Cabell.

"It was Painter," repeated Muirdyke. He put one hand firmly on the table, palm down, indicating that the matter was closed. "I'll put it up to the inspector next time I see him."

"You did already," said Edwina.

"Eh? No, I didn't. I just said he had a grudge — What's that?"

Someone was pounding on the front door, loud enough to be heard in the dining room. Whoever it was must have been admitted, for the pounding stopped and was replaced by indistinct but plainly angry shouting in the hall.

Pembert entered. "Sir, there is a person —"

"Never mind announcing me, cocky," said the newcomer, thrusting past Pembert and revealing himself to be a burly individual, black of hair and whisker and incongruously dressed in a purple suit and yellow shoes. "I'm here to see Muirdyke."

"*Mister* Muirdyke to you, Egg," said Muirdyke, standing up.

"Oh, we *are* grand," sneered Egg. "All right then, *Mister* Muirdyke. Felton hasn't heard from you and he'd like to know why."

"Felton wants to hear from me? Right-ho. You can go back and tell him three things: one, his money's safe; two, I'm doing no more business with him; and three, if he thinks he can send toughs into gentleman's houses and get away with it, he'll find he's very much mistaken!"

"That's your answer?"

"It is."

The two men traded challenging stares. Egg took a step toward

Muirdyke; Cabell stood up. Faced with two fit men and a (clearly unintimidated) young woman as witness, Egg stopped and said, "I'll tell him. The next time, though, words won't be enough. Gentlemen's houses, is it? *Gentlemen* don't welsh on their bets. When I come back — you'd better have the monkey!"

He left. Muirdyke took a deep breath, leaned on the table for a moment to steady himself, and sat down. He poured himself another glass of wine and drank it off. "Well, that was dashed awkward," he remarked.

"Who was that?" asked Edwina. "And who is Felton?"

"Felton's a bookmaker," said Charles. "And that was Egg."

"*Egg?*" asked Edwina.

"Felton's collector," replied Muirdyke. "His name — dashed posh name for a tough — is Eggleston Harbaugh. If one of Felton's customers is a little slow paying up, Felton sends Egg to pay him a visit."

"And you are a little slow in paying up the — monkey?" asked Cabell.

"That's slang for five hundred pounds, and yes, I've been a little slow. But now I'll be able to pay — I say, that's put me in a bit of a spot, what? If the inspector finds out I'm in a hole —"

"You'd better tell him yourself," said Edwina.

"Really? I suppose I should… Dash it all, must I?"

"Yes," said Edwina. "You can tell him about Painter while you're there."

"Right, then. I'll go to Fenchester first thing tomorrow." Muirdyke poured himself another glass of wine.

"May I borrow Pembert after dinner?" asked Edwina. "I'd like to start my sketching."

"Of course. What do you say to a walk down to the Wyvern first?"

"With Egg hanging about?"

"Oh, dash Egg. We can get there and back without him seeing us. There's a way — used to do it whenever Uncle Sebastian had been down on me more than usual about drinking. As soon as he was in his study — out the window from the drawing room, round to the back, down to the High Road where it curves close to the manor, cut back up to the village and in at the rear of the pub. Just had to be sure I was back before ten. Shall we go?"

"Thanks, but I'd like to get to work."

"Right-ho."

Dinner over, Edwina went to the library and sent for Pembert. As soon as he arrived, she briskly sat him down, attached a large sheet of sketch paper to the easel, took up a new stick of charcoal and set to work. As she went on she felt a growing sense of unease, so after only ten minutes later she put down the charcoal and stepped back to gauge the overall effect.

The sketch was a study in misery. Looking at the man himself, it was clear to Edwina the sketch was accurate. *How did I miss it? Am I keen-sighted as an artist but blind as a fellow-human?*

"Why, Pembert!" she exclaimed. "What's the matter?"

"It's all just too much," moaned Pembert. "I cannot stand it." The whole story poured out of him: how he had been convicted of forgery and been in prison; how he had thought it behind him when he came to work at the manor; how he had regained peace and self-respect as he found himself trusted and justifying that trust; and how the inspector had found him out. Intermixed with this was grief at the death of Mr. Oldfield and the feeling that somehow he had failed in his duty by allowing it to happen. "And now everyone will know, and even if Mr. Charles stays on I shan't be able to hold my head up for the disgrace. And I'm sure the inspector suspects me and I shall be arrested for murder and hanged. Perhaps that would be best — I'd be better off dead!"

"None of that, Pembert. Pull yourself together!" said Edwina. "I don't believe you killed Mr. Oldfield. When Mr. Muirdyke gets back we shall go to him and tell him the truth — it will be better hearing it from you than from the police. If Mr. Oldfield and Mr. Cabell could keep it to themselves, so can he. And the next time I see the inspector I'll give him a rocket for suspecting you — and let's have nothing more about you being better off hanged, not when it lets the real murderer get away with it."

"Thank you, Miss Hackett," said the butler, tears in his eyes and his voice quivering with emotion.

"We'll try again tomorrow when you're more composed. Could you please find out if anyone else on the staff is free and send them to me?"

Edwina considered tearing up the portrait, but could not bring herself to do so; it was, after all, one of the best things she had done. She decided to take it with her when she left Minstrel Manor.

Soon William arrived, excited to be sketched.

Muirdyke dropped into the library in search of a thriller shortly after Edwina finished a portrait of Hannah, the cook, who had come after William. Seeing the light on in the studio he ambled over. "Hullo, Miss Hackett — hard at work, I see. May I take a look?" Muirdyke went to stand behind Edwina. "That's a dashed good likeness. I don't know how you artists do it." He caught sight of the portrait of William which she had laid on the table to her left and picked it up for a better look. "Amazing." Beneath William was the sketch of Pembert. "I say, you've made Pembert a bit down in the mouth. I didn't know he'd be so broken up over Uncle Sebastian."

"It's not just that," said Edwina. "But it's best if you hear it from Pembert himself."

"Right." Muirdyke went out of the studio and used the library telephone to summon the butler.

When Pembert arrived Edwina took him aside. "I've told Mr. Muirdyke you have something to say to him."

"N – now?" faltered the butler.

"You may as well get it over with. Would you rather I left you alone with him?"

"Oh, no, Miss Hackett. Please stay."

"Of course. Don't worry — everything will be fine." They returned to Muirdyke, who was nonchalantly half-sitting on a corner of one of the tables. Pembert stood before him, Edwina at his side. "Go on," she encouraged.

"Well, Mr. Charles," began Pembert, and went on with his story. Muirdyke listened with no change of expression. At the end of the tale he took a deep breath and let it out in a long soft whistle. "How dashed unpleasant," he said. The butler's face fell. "Unpleasant for you, I mean."

"You'll keep him on, of course?" said Edwina.

"Good Lord, yes." Muirdyke stood up and clapped Pembert on the shoulder. "It'd be a dashed poor show to kick you out. Uncle Sebastian trusted you — that's all I need to know." Pembert turned away, brought out a handkerchief, and mopped his eyes. Muirdyke picked up the telephone receiver. "Is that you, William? Bring some port to the library — and three glasses."

"I'll come with you to Fenchester tomorrow," said Edwina. "I want to have a word with the inspector."

ART TO FIND THE MIND'S CONSTRUCTION IN THE FACE

Thursday morning came, greyer and more dismal than Wednesday. "There's more snow coming," remarked Mallow to Bellman, "or I'm a Dutchman."

"Where are we going today?" asked the sergeant.

"Chiltonbury, at least, to visit Merryweather's bank. We have an appointment to meet the manager at 11:30. We can bypass the manor — we'll meet Cabell and Miss Hackett at the inquest and can question them then." Mallow removed his spectacles and rubbed his eyes. "As things have turned out, the inquest is set for a damned inconvenient time. We should be finished in Chiltonbury well before it starts and then we either hang about there for a few hours or come back here and then go back to Minstrel Folly... Maybe it would be better to go to the manor after all."

Constable Pyke came into Mallow's office and at the same time his telephone rang. Mallow picked up the receiver. "Inspector?" came the voice of Sergeant Daw. "A Mr. Charles Muirdyke just rang up, from Minstrel Manor. He said he's coming here to see you this morning, as he has a statement to make."

"Damn him," said Mallow. "He could just as well have stayed there. We'll see him at the inquest. Did he say when?"

"Only that he would be leaving at once, and then he rang off."

Mallow thanked the sergeant and hung up. "Wasting our time," he grumbled to Bellman. "Now we have to wait until Muirdyke arrives." He glanced at the clock. "Eight-thirty. If he doesn't take too long, we can still get to the bank on time. No stopping at the manor, then. Pyke, there's something you can do. Find Porlock and send him out to whichever newsagent he visited yesterday and see if the back issue of the *Panopticon* has arrived."

Soon Porlock arrived, bringing Pyke and the magazine with him. "Good," remarked Mallow, putting on his spectacles again. "Now we can find out what the murderer didn't want us to see."

"If it was the murderer, sir," said Pyke.

"Yes, yes," replied Mallow, already scanning the pages. "Nothing — nothing — *this* looks interesting. 'Society Murders, No. 6: The Hon. Mary Callender.'" He read on. "Daughter of Lord Trevane. Married one Robert Callender, who killed her in December of 1912 during a quarrel about her debts. Callender disappeared, leaving a note in which he admitted his guilt and his intention to kill himself. His body was never found. Hullo, it says here Callender was employed as a technician at a glassworks. Wasn't Oldfield's first invention some special kind of glass?" He turned back a page and handed the magazine to Bellman. "What do you make of that?"

"Of what?" asked Bellman.

"At the head of the article. There are cuts of Robert and Mary Callender. Look at Robert."

Bellman studied the illustration carefully. The countenance was of a stout, dark-haired young man with a quizzical eyebrow. "I don't make anything of it."

"Oh, of course, you never saw the painting. You did, Pyke. What do you think?"

"I can't be sure, sir," said Pyke. "It's not a photograph. But there *is* a resemblance to Oldfield."

"Are you suggesting Oldfield was Callender?" asked Bellman. "And faked his suicide?"

"It's a possibility, no more," replied Mallow. "But it ought to be followed up — as if we didn't have enough already."

"But how would that fit in with his murder?"

"I don't know, but — what the hell, let's indulge in a little speculation," said Mallow. "We've nothing better to do at the moment. We've already suspected Oldfield was being blackmailed. Here's an excellent reason why."

"Or someone found out who he was, and killed him to avenge Mary Callender," suggested Pyke.

"If I may say so, Pyke's idea is sounder than yours, sir," said Bellman. "The *victim* of a blackmailer doesn't usually end up dead — it's the other way round. And if it was a revenge killing — the killer would have wanted to avoid us making the connection with Callender. That's why he tore out the issue."

"We'll have to ask Cabell about this, too," said Mallow. "He met Oldfield in — when was it?"

"1913," said Pyke.

"1913. Not long afterwards. Oldfield might have let something slip."

"Aren't we getting ahead of ourselves?" asked Bellman.

Mallow sighed. "You're right. Fun and games, but they don't get us any farther. Go look busy, you two." He retrieved the magazine from Pyke. "I'll give this a thorough read-through and see if anything else ties in. Pyke, I'll want you when Muirdyke arrives." His telephone rang. "Yes?"

"Call from Scotland Yard, sir," said Daw.

"Put it through."

"Inspector Mallow? This is Jarvis, of Records. You had asked for information about a Barnabas Merryweather? I'm sorry, sir, but that name is not in our files."

"Thank you. We'll have to track him down ourselves, then. I've another request for you. Can you look up the file on the murder of the Honourable Mary Callender in 1912?"

"Yes, sir."

"Thank you again." Mallow put down the receiver and the telephone rang again. "Yes?"

"Good morning, George."

"Oh! Good morning, Superintendent."

"I read your report. You're making progress."

"Am I, sir? It doesn't feel like it."

"You're getting pieces to the puzzle. Enough pieces and you'll be able to start putting them together."

"I hope so, sir. We may have a new one, but it's very uncertain and may not come to anything."

"Let me know if it does. I spoke with Carstairs: his men will be looking for this Merryweather fellow. Oh, and the Yard called. They're sending down an expert to open the safe. He's arriving on the 1:15 today."

"Bellman and I are going to Chiltonbury this morning. We'll meet him at the manor."

"Will you have time to look in the safe before the inquest?"

"I think so. The inquest isn't until four."

"And if you find anything, will you bring it up?"

"No. I expect we'll call the minimum of evidence. We don't want to confuse the jury."

"Good hunting."

"Thank you, sir." Mallow looked at the clock again. It was 8:45.

Muirdyke and Edwina did not arrive until 9:15. Mallow spent the intervening time getting up from his desk and pacing back and forth, looking out the window, sitting down again and re-reading the Callender article, and checking the clock every minute or two. When Pyke brought them into his office, he greeted them, sat them down, and came at once to the point. "You have something to tell me, Mr. Muirdyke?" he asked.

"Yes. I thought it best, Inspector, to add to the information I gave you yesterday," said Muirdyke.

"Go on."

"I came down from London for the purpose of asking my uncle for five hundred pounds. I owe that sum to a bookmaker named Felton, who is growing impatient."

"I see."

"I don't want you to think I've been concealing anything."

"Of course not. Is that all?"

"No. I think you should take a very close look at Silas Painter."

"You have already mentioned him. Do you have any new information about him?"

"Well — no. But I'm convinced he did it." Muirdyke propounded his theory, closing with a recommendation to examine the handle of Painter's stick for traces of blood.

"Thank you, Mr. Muirdyke," said Mallow. "I can assure you we are looking at Silas Painter — and everyone else concerned with this case."

"I know you are," burst out Edwina. "Well you can just stop looking at Pembert! You've been hounding him about that one crime he committed years and years ago — for which he's paid — and now you're planning to arrest him for the murder of Mr. Oldfield! The poor man is half out of his mind with worry. It's just not possible he did it!"

"How do you know that, Miss Hackett," asked Mallow. "What haven't you told me?"

"I should have thought it was as plain as a pikestaff. All you have to do is *talk* to the man and you'll see he's utterly incapable of hurting anyone."

"*That's* your evidence, Miss Hackett? You should study crime more closely. There's many a cold-blooded murder that has been committed by a man or woman who seemed as harmless as Pembert — until it was brought home to them.

"And I should like to know where you got your ideas of what we're doing. Yes, I confronted Pembert with his past — once. There's some indication forgery plays a part in this case. It would have been negligent not to follow up a possible motive."

"There's another reason —"

Mallow rode over her. "I will not say who we may or may not suspect at this point. But I *will* say I would as soon arrest you as Pembert — and maybe sooner. Why didn't you tell me your father worked for Mr. Oldfield, and was sacked after quarreling with him?"

Edwina's eyes widened in surprise. "How — how did you find out?"

"I visited Mr. Oldfield's shop in Swannington yesterday and spoke with a man who remembered you — Harry Bledsoe."

"Harry Bledsoe! He's still there? I liked him. There was another man, who smoked a pipe, that I didn't like as much — I don't recall *his* name." Edwina frowned as she tried to remember.

"Attkinson?"

Edwina's face cleared. "That's the one."

"So you knew your father worked there?"

"Yes — and no. I didn't know it was Mr. Oldfield's shop until yesterday, when I recognised Mr. Cabell. So you think I might have killed Mr. Oldfield because he sacked Dad —" Edwina counted on her fingers "— seven years ago? That's silly."

"The strength of a motive depends on who has it, Miss Hackett." Mallow turned to Muirdyke. "Mr. Muirdyke, as long as you're here, I have one or two questions for you. Is the name Robert Callender familiar to you?"

"Not that I can remember," said Muirdyke. He caught sight of the magazine on Mallow's desk. "Hold on — yes, I do. You see, I used to read to Uncle Sebastian when he had one of his migraines. A few months back there was a story — it was in that issue of the *Panopticon*, the one you have there — about this Callender chap, the one that killed his wife. He sat straight up when he heard the title. Made me read it twice."

"Did he say why he was interested?"

"No. But he told me to go away afterwards — said he needed to think."

Edwina, intrigued, said "May I?" Without waiting for an answer she picked up the magazine and started reading the article in question.

Mallow went on. "Did anything else in that issue interest him, or did he react like that any other time you were reading to him?"

"No."

"One other question. Did your uncle ever mention a man named Barnabas Merryweather?"

Muirdyke thought for a few moments before replying "Oh, yes."

"In what connection?"

"He was a character in one of the plays my uncle liked to recite — *The Virtuous Villain,* it was. One of Uncle Sebastian's favorites. He loved Victorian melodrama. He used to say he'd walk ten miles in the snow to see a good old blood-and-thunder performance with lots of ranting and carrying on, but he wouldn't go into the next room to see Shaw or Ibsen. Anyhow, there's this cove, Merryweather, and for most of the play you think he's the heavy, but in the last act he turns the tables on the real one."

"A character in a play?" asked Mallow. "Not a real person?"

"Good Lord, no," replied Muirdyke. "I mean, who'd want to go around calling himself a name like that?"

"Someone has. Your uncle was paying him money. A great deal of money — six thousand pounds in all. You're sure he never spoke of this man?"

"Quite sure. How dashed odd. I must ask Cabell about it."

"Mr. Cabell has told us he doesn't know anything about it."

"That's even odder. Cabell always handled Uncle Sebastian's money matters. Is there anything else?"

"Not at the moment, Mr. Muirdyke. Miss Hackett, *may* I have that back — when you're quite finished with it?

"What?" replied Edwina, without looking up. "Oh, yes — I'm almost done."

"Sir," said Pyke, "may I ask Mr. Muirdyke a question?"

"Go ahead."

"Mr. Muirdyke, what was your mother's maiden name?"

"Eh? What a dashed silly question. Oldfield, of course."

"Thank you, sir." Pyke glanced at Mallow, who was staring at him, and shrugged in apology.

"There — finished," said Edwina. She put the *Panopticon* on Mallow's desk. "Do you have any more questions for *me*, Inspector?"

"No. Yes. Where did you go yesterday?"

"I drove Mr. Cabell into Fenchester so that he could pick up his car at the railway station. Then I went on the Kympole to pick up some things at my cottage."

"I distinctly remember asking you not to leave the neighbourhood of the manor. Did you forget this?"

"Certainly not. Naturally, I took it to mean I shouldn't go and stay somewhere else, and I haven't. I didn't realise you were putting me under house arrest."

Mallow's temper flared. "That is *not* —" he began, then caught himself and counted ten. Regaining his composure, he went on, "Perhaps I could have been clearer. From now on, please continue at the manor. If you must go somewhere, please ring us up here and let us know. You both may go."

When Edwina and Muirdyke had gone, Mallow said, "Pyke – don't make a habit of showing up your superiors like that."

"Sorry, sir."

"Don't apologise. That was a damned fatuous idea I had, and I'm glad it was exploded before I made a fool of myself over it. Still, now we know there *is* a connection between Oldfield and Callender, and it's likely the murderer wanted to conceal it... Meanwhile, I have some questions to ask in Chiltonbury. There's a safe-cracking expert from the Yard coming on the 1:15. Meet him at the station and bring him to the manor." He looked at the clock, which now read five minutes to ten. "Blast, we're going to be late. Where's Bellman?"

~

"The inspector's an ass," said Muirdyke when they were outside head-quarters. "Suspecting you, suspecting Pembert —"

"Now I've cooled off, I can see he's within his rights," replied Edwina. "After all, I did say last night Pembert and I were the obvious suspects."

"Well, yes," grudged Muirdyke. "I suppose I am too, now I've told him about Felton. Who'll he suspect next? Cabell, I suppose, and William, and a burglar, and Joe from the Wyvern, and Uncle Tom Cobley and all, until finally he gets round to Painter... I wonder what put him on to Callender? And who's this chappie pretending to be Merryweather?"

"I'm sure it will all come out in the end. He found out about Dad quickly enough. Made my rocket fizzle, rather."

Muirdyke waved the fizzle aside. "I say, I need a little pick-me-up after all those questions. Let's drop into the Goose and Feathers for a quick one before we go back to the manor."

"Oh, bother, there was something I didn't tell him," said Edwina. She turned to go back.

"Never mind. I'm sure we'll see him again. Come on. There's some pretty good beer at the Goose."

~

Before they reached Swannington, Muirdyke decided he wanted to stop there and see Henry Radford about getting Felton's five hundred pounds. Edwina waited in his car, alone with her thoughts. *I wonder who the inspector really suspects. Could it be me? It's one thing as an intellectual game around the dinner table, but for real?* Her imagination cast up vivid scenes: Inspector Mallow coming to her and saying, "Edwina Hackett, I arrest you on the charge of murdering Sebastian Oldfield. Anything you say shall be taken down and used as evidence..." Her own protestations of innocence ignored. The trial — the judge putting on the black cap — her last sight the hangman's noose. *Don't be a silly goose, Edwina. They haven't any evidence.*

She didn't see Muirdyke come out of Mr. Radford's office and beckon to her. He stood for a moment, waiting, and then called out "Hoy — Miss Hackett!" She looked up and he beckoned again. She got out of the car and joined him.

"What's up?" she asked. "Did you get the money?"

"I did *not*," replied Muirdyke, giving a lump of frozen slush a vicious kick. "He said I can't touch a penny until the will is proved. I had to tell him why I wanted the money, and he said that while he'd be willing to advance me fifty pounds or so on his own responsibility, he certainly wouldn't go to five hundred and especially not for such a reason. I gather he'd heard this and that about me from Uncle Sebastian — he started sermonizing about the vice of gambling. Then he got onto the evils of alcohol and I walked out."

"What are you going to do?"

"Drop into the Gilded Newt for another quick one. Evils of alcohol, indeed. Damn his eyes!"

"I meant about the money."

"I don't know. Go to ground at the manor, I suppose, until the will *is* proved. Hire a bally bodyguard in case Egg shows up again. Or maybe Uncle Sebastian had a gun about the place somewhere — I'll have to ask Cabell."

The quick one at the Gilded Newt turned into a not-so-quick three. When they left, Edwina, who had had her one at the Goose and Feathers and since confined herself to lemon squashes, felt a qualm as she watched an unsteady Muirdyke get behind the wheel.

"Maybe you'd better let me drive?" she suggested.

"No, no," replied Muirdyke. "I'm fine."

In the first mile they had close calls with a stray sheep, a van, and a man on a bicycle.

"Stop the car," commanded Edwina.

Muirdyke obliged. "Why?"

"I'm getting out. I'll walk the rest of the way."

"Oh, all right, I can take a hint as well as the next fellah. You drive."

After a few minutes of silence, Edwina tried to lighten the atmosphere. "I'm doing a portrait of Mr. Cabell. I want to do one of you as well. When would be a good time for you?"

"A portrait of me? I'd like to see that. How about this afternoon?"

Upon their return they found the summonses to the inquest waiting for them. "You, me, Mr. Cabell, and Pembert," said Edwina, looking through them. "Oh, and William too. This will be interesting. I've never been to an inquest before. What do you suppose will happen?"

"Lord knows," replied Muirdyke. "If this were a book, the inspector will spring a surprise on us. It all depends on what he's found out so far."

After lunch Edwina and Muirdyke went to the library but found Cabell already in the studio, looking at Mr. Oldfield's portrait. "Oh, dear," said Edwina. "I forgot I'd already arranged to sketch Mr. Cabell at this time."

"Oh, that's all right," replied Muirdyke. "I'll just pop down to the Wyvern. When do you think you'll be done?"

"I don't know. It may go smoothly or it may not. Perhaps you could come back in an hour?"

"Right-ho."

Cabell placed himself in the sitter's chair. Edwina carefully removed the painting from the easel, pinned up a sheet of sketch paper, and stared at Cabell for a minute or two before taking up the charcoal and setting to work.

She worked briskly at first, but soon her strokes became slower and more tentative. Twice she stopped and looked frowningly at Cabell. Finally she put down the charcoal with a sigh, unpinned the sketch, and crumpled it up.

"It's not working," said Edwina. "I'm not getting a read from you — you have the most impenetrable face I've ever seen. I'm not doing a portrait — I'm doing a still life. You should be sitting between a fancy goblet and a bunch of grapes."

"There's no art to find the mind's construction in the face," said Cabell. Seeing Edwina's incomprehension, he added, "Shakespeare."

"Oh! *Hamlet,* isn't it?"

"Macbeth."

"Close enough."

"If it will help, I should be happy to fetch a goblet — I don't know if we have any fancy ones —and some grapes. Perhaps a loaf of bread and a salmon on a silver plate as well?"

"I've just learned something about you I didn't know — you have a sense of humour. That helps. Please keep talking while I'm working — I often get something from my subjects that way."

"What should I talk about?"

"Anything you like. It's not so much what you say that's important — it's how you say it."

Edwina began again on a fresh sheet of paper. Cabell spoke at first at random of trivial topics and gradually drifted into reminiscences of his work with Oldfield, speaking with pride — almost boasting — of the discoveries they had made.

At the end of forty-five minutes, Edwina stepped back and pronounced the sketch finished. Cabell came over and looked at it for a long while.

"Do you know, old Duncan was wrong," he said at last.

"Duncan?"

"The character who said the line I quoted before. He was speaking of the Thane of Cawdor."

"Oh?" said Edwina, whose knowledge of Shakespeare was confined to a few of the better-known lines from *Hamlet.* She stared at the portrait. "I think I got some of you — I just don't know what it is."

Cabell did not reply at first. Finally he said, "It's loneliness. I spent fourteen years working at Oldfield's side, helping to make his dreams real. Now he's gone and I realise no one has been at *my* side and whatever dreams I may have had are dreams still. I have been a lonely man — Edwina. We haven't known each other long and I'm rather older than you, but —"

Edwina, shaken, cut him off. "I'm very sorry, Mr. Cabell, but that is quite out of the question. I'm happy with the way my life is going at present and I have no wish to change it."

"Ah," said Cabell. "I see. Forgive my forwardness."

"There's nothing to forgive," said Edwina. "I — I appreciate the compliment."

"Well," said Cabell, "I shall not go away with nothing. There is still the portrait."

"I'm afraid you'll have to wait a day or two," said Edwina, glad to move the conversation to familiar ground. "I still have to fix it and cut a matte to fit it."

"I shall practise patience," said Cabell, and made a dignified exit.

"Oh, dear," said Edwina out loud. She began reflecting on her words to Cabell. She had been taken by surprise, and had said the first thing that came to her; but, she concluded, it had been the truth. Marriage was not something she had ever seriously considered. *It's all right for Dot and Rodney — they suit each other. I wonder what sort of man would suit me — or I, him? No time to think about it. I have work to do.*

She picked up a cloth and looked again at the sketch. While rubbing smears of charcoal from her hands, she realised she had come away from her cottage without any shellac. *Oh, bother, now I'll have to go back again. Wait a moment — did Mr. Oldfield use it at all? There may be some in the workshop.* Hoping to catch Cabell, she left the studio and nearly ran into Muirdyke.

"There you are," said Muirdyke. "Finished with Cabell?"

"Yes. Come into the studio."

"Right-ho."

Muirdyke settled into the sitter's chair, and Edwina once again set to work. The sketch was soon done. If there were any hidden depths in Muirdyke, Edwina had not perceived them.

"I say — is that really me?" he asked, examining the finished product.

"Well — I think it's pretty close."

"Good Lord, he's rather a poor sort of cove, isn't he?"

"Oh, I don't know. I might have been influenced by your behaviour today."

"Oh?"

"I don't want to sermonise like Mr. Radford, but you have been drinking a lot."

"Oh, I say — have I?"

"Yes."

"And that's what you think of me?"

"It's not what *I* think. It's what the artist in me sees in the subject and puts down. If you'll pardon my saying so, the subject doesn't *have* to stay that way. He might turn out quite well when — or if — he grows up."

"You know," said Muirdyke slowly, "a cove might grow up pretty fast if he had a good reason — and if he had someone there to encourage him — maybe even a little advice now and then —"

Oh dear, is this going to happen every time? "No doubt," interrupted Edwina. "And I trust in time he'll find the right someone. Now, if you don't mind, I have some tidying up to do."

"Right-ho," said Muirdyke, turning to go. He turned back. Edwina was cleaning her hands again. "I say, you missed a spot or two."

"Oh?" replied Edwina. She looked at her hands. "Where?"

"Just above your right eyebrow."

"Bother," said Edwina, rubbing at the indicated spot.

"And your right cheek."

"Thank you."

"You also have charcoal in your hair."

"Really? Oh, well, it washes out."

"Right-ho," said Muirdyke again, and finally left.

What a day, thought Edwina when she was alone, and it's only a quarter past two. She went upstairs for a bath and a bit of a cry. Coming downstairs and crossing the hall afterwards she nearly collided with Pembert, who was carrying a tray holding a bottle of brandy and a glass.

"Brandy in the afternoon?" she asked. "Is someone ill?"

"It's for Mr. Charles in the billiard room," replied Pembert.

"Oh, dear. I hope he remembers the inquest is in a couple of hours." Edwina passed on to the library and sat down to Oldfield's portrait.

Was I too hard on him? I don't think so. The sketch is what it is. I can't help it if that's what I saw. Or was it being turned down? Was it that big a blow? But I couldn't say anything else. Oh, bother, bother, bother...

13

GO AWAY AND LET ME DO MY JOB

The city of Chiltonbury, in West Fenshire, had once been the chief municipality of the shire. Located at the highest navigable point of the River Culver, it was a natural centre for trade. The Earls of Fenshire had derived a goodly revenue from tolls and rents there; when the earls were no more, affairs fell into the hands of the Maunder and Edgbaston families. The flow of money ceased when the silting-up of the river above Fenchester caused most of the traffic to move to that town, which eventually surpassed Chiltonbury in importance. The coming of the railways ended any hope the latter could regain its predominance, for the Great Northern Railway (since renamed the London and North Eastern Railway) was built through Fenchester. The city still prided itself on its capacious Market Square, several well-designed terraces, crescents, and walks, and on the cathedral, which was one of the grandest in England; and Fenchester still lay in the Diocese of Chiltonbury.

Stopping just long enough at the headquarters of the West Fenshire police to report to Superintendent Carstairs and procure a warrant, Mallow proceeded to the bank of Maunder & Co., just off the Market Square. He was soon closeted with Morris Hanscombe, the manager, a bald little man with bushy black eyebrows and gold pince-nez perched on a long sharp nose. "I remember this Merryweather," he said. "I met him when he opened the account. He had a letter from Sebastian Oldfield. Excuse me a moment." He went to the door, opened it, and called out, "Henderson, bring me the Merryweather file. What? Unlikely there's more than one, but this one is *Barnabas* Merryweather." He came back to his desk. "It's a very odd thing — very odd. When I met him, I thought I'd seen him before somewhere."

"Where — here in Chiltonbury? And when?"

"No, that's what makes it so odd. I thought I'd seen him before the War — several years before, when I was a young man."

"Perhaps he merely reminded you of someone?"

"No, no. The name, Barnabas Merryweather, and the man — they went together."

"In a play, perhaps?" asked Bellman.

"That's it! A play — damned foolish stuff it was, too. A girl I was going with at the time dragged me to it. She liked that sort of thing; had a bit of a crush on the hero, too."

The Merryweather file arrived. There was the letter, signed "Sebastian Oldfield". It merely recommended Barnabas Merryweather to Maunder & Co. as a trustworthy client and asked all correspondence be sent to him care of Sebastian Oldfield at Minstrel Manor. Mallow looked it over and handed it to Bellman.

"Did you verify the letter?"

"Yes. I rang up Mr. Oldfield and spoke with him myself. He assured me the letter was genuine. But why is there any doubt? Mr. Oldfield's bank has been accepting the cheques."

"I did not say there was any doubt, sir," said Mallow. "We are merely trying to find Mr. Merryweather. If any correspondence addressed to or from him arrives, please let me know. Here's my card. And if he should come in, please inform him the police would very much like to meet with him."

"Of course."

"Can you tell me the current balance of Mr. Merryweather's account?"

"Certainly." Hanscombe left and returned a few minutes later. "The balance is five thousand, nine hundred and fifty pounds."

"There's one other thing, sir. May I borrow this letter long enough to take it to the police station and have a photostatic copy made?"

"No need for that, Inspector. We can copy it here with our own machine. Maunder & Co. prides itself on being up-to-date." Bellman returned the letter to Hanscombe, who took it off to be copied.

"Why get a photostatic copy, sir?" asked Bellman. "The letter was straightforward enough."

"Didn't you see?" asked Mallow. "The letter was in one hand-writing and the signature was in another. I want to compare them both with the cheques and with the document found in Oldfield's study… So Merryweather has left almost all the money in his account. That's a blow to the blackmail theory. I wonder what he wanted the fifty pounds for."

Furnished with the copy, they left the bank. The day had grown darker and a chill wind swept along the street. "Brrr!" said Mallow, buttoning his overcoat and wrapping his muffler more tightly about himself. "I loathe cold weather."

"*Blow, blow, thou winter wind, thou art not so unkind as man's ingratitude,*" said Bellman.

"Eh?" replied Mallow, taken aback. "Feeling unappreciated, Sergeant?"

"Oh, no, sir," Bellman hastened to reply. "Just a quotation — Shakespeare."

"*The Winter's Tale* again, I suppose?"

"No, sir; *As You Like It.*"

"Well, I don't like it. Let's find a place where we can get a hot meal and then back to the manor for a look inside the safe. The way this case is going, there could be anything in there from a rajah's ruby to a stuffed hedgehog."

At Minstrel Manor they were admitted by Pembert. As soon as they were inside, he said, "I have something to tell you, Inspector."

"What is it? But first, is there somewhere we can talk where I can be sure Miss Hackett isn't listening in?"

"Miss Hackett, I understand, is at work in her studio. Perhaps the drawing room would be best."

In the drawing room Pembert began. "You asked me yesterday if Mr. Oldfield had had any dealings with a man named Merryweather. He had, but in my agitation I forgot. Last year — I believe it was in August — Mr. Oldfield asked me to write a letter for him, as he had accidentally burnt his hand with acid and was unable to write. The letter was to Maunder & Co. in Chiltonbury recommending Mr. Merryweather, who wished to open an account there."

"Indeed?" replied Mallow. He produced the copy he had obtained at the bank. "Is this the letter?"

Pembert looked it over. "Yes, it is. Mr. Oldfield also instructed me, and the rest of the staff, that any telephone calls from Maunder & Co., or from the Bank of Fenshire, whether the main office or the branch in Swannington, should be put through to him instead of Mr. Cabell. If he was with Mr. Cabell we were to say he was unavailable and to take a message."

"Mr. Cabell used to take such calls?"

"Mr. Cabell took all business calls. He still does, apart from those from the banks."

"What about the post?"

"Mr. Oldfield gave instructions about that also," said Pembert. "Either William or I took in the post each day. In the past we had taken it to Mr. Cabell. Mr. Oldfield directed we should bring it to him first."

"Thank you, Pembert. You may go; and please, do not repeat this conversation to anyone. Oh — I should tell you a Mr. Thomas

Marjoram will be arriving here this afternoon to help us with our investigations. We'll be waiting for him in the study."

"Yes, sir."

"Well, Bellman," said Mallow when they were alone in the study, "what does it sound like to you?"

"It looks straightforward enough. Oldfield didn't want Cabell to know of his dealings with Merryweather; or at least the details."

"I agree." Mallow looked at his watch. "The expert won't be here for some time yet. We forgot to experiment with the door yesterday — let's give it a try."

The experiment confirmed it was impossible to get from the desk through the door before it closed. Bellman, not wishing to risk injury to a book, took two of the magazines from the reading table and used them to block the door from closing completely. They found, however, that even the united effort of two men could not move it a single inch.

Presently Pembert ushered into the study a portly man, his waved brown hair shot with grey. With them came Constable Pyke, who introduced the newcomer as the expert from the Yard.

"Thomas Marjoram, at your service," said the expert. "Once a burglar and cracksman, since converted to law and order, sweetness and light. What can I do for you, Inspector?"

"Have you ever opened an Oldfield book-safe?" asked Mallow.

Marjoram's eyes brightened. "No, sir," he replied. "I've never even heard of them. By George, I haven't seen a new kind of safe in years. You've made my day."

Mallow pointed out the safe to Marjoram and the ex-burglar set to work. For an hour he poked, prodded, sounded, probed, and manipulated, while the inspector looked on with growing impatience. To add to his irritation, Edwina drifted in to watch.

Finally Marjoram confessed defeat. "I hate to admit this," he said.

"This safe is something else. I've tried everything I know, but it's got me beat. You'll need a diamond drill, or even gelignite, to get into it, and I don't have either with me."

"I don't think gelignite is quite the proper tool here," said Mallow.

"We could ask Cabell," suggested Bellman.

"Don't you remember? Cabell said only Oldfield knew the combination."

"I don't suppose he'd have written it down anywhere?"

"Doubtful. If his memory was as good as Cabell said it was, he wouldn't need to."

"Inspector?" said Edwina.

This was the last straw for Mallow. "Damn it, Edwina, will you go away and let me do my job!" he barked. *Oh, God, in front of everybody.* He tried to get out an apology but was tongue-tied.

Edwina was undaunted. "I wanted to say — George — I think I can open the safe for you."

"What?"

"Dad worked on that invention. When he took me to the shop with him, he let me play with some of the things he was working on, at least the less dangerous ones. This was one of them. The way it works is that you have to press the backs of the books in a particular order, which is set by whoever uses the safe. It's really just another kind of combination lock."

"I'll be blessed," said Marjoram. "I never thought of that."

"You mean your father set the combination for this safe and told you what it was?" asked Mallow.

"No. Dad loved to tinker with Mr. Oldfield's inventions, and he built a master combination into the design. One of our games was for Dad to set a combination and then let me override it. I loved that game and we played it over and over. I'm pretty sure I can still remember the master."

Mallow sighed. "Oh, very well — give it a try."

Edwina went to the bookshelves and knelt down in front of the safe. The others crowded around and watched with interest. She frowned in concentration as her fingers began an intricate dance along the backs of the books. At its conclusion she grasped the top edge and pulled.

Nothing happened.

"Bother," said Edwina, "I got it wrong. Let's try again." This time she closed her eyes and held out her hands, going back into the past. Then the dance started again. Mallow, watching closely, could not see what she did differently, but when the dance ended there was a loud click. Edwina pulled and the safe opened.

Marjoram began applauding but after a moment realised no one else was, and stopped.

If Mallow *had* been expecting a rajah's ruby, or even a stuffed hedgehog, he would have been disappointed. But as he was merely expecting the unexpected, he was amply rewarded.

Item: Six canceled cheques, made out to Barnabas Merryweather, each for £1,000.

Item: A suit of clothes, rather old-fashioned, including a blue coat and a plaid vest.

Item: A pair of plain-glass spectacles.

Item: A red wig and false side-whiskers.

Item: An ebony stick with a silver handle in the shape of a basilisk's head.

Item: A bundle of old playbills.

Item: Another bundle, of old newspaper clippings.

Item: An envelope, labeled "Crosby & Co. / Gold / 1 oz (Troy)." It contained a small piece of bright yellow metal.

Handling everything carefully, to avoid disturbing any fingerprints, Mallow took them from the safe and laid them out on the floor, as the desk had not been cleaned since his first visit. The remains of Oldfield's last meal were spotted with mould, the spilled butter had spread farther, almost to the edge, and fingerprint powder lay scattered everywhere.

He looked first at the playbills. The earliest was dated 15 April 1894; the latest, 24 June 1912. All advertised plays acted by the

Holborn Repertory Company, among them *Richard III; Macbeth; Titus Andronicus; Sweeney Todd the Barber; The Druid's Revenge; Captured by Pirates; The Virtuous Villain.* Among the regular players was listed "S. Oldfield". In *The Virtuous Villain* he played a character named "Barnabas Merryweather."

The newspaper clippings were reviews of performances by the company. All mentioned "S. Oldfield" or "Sebastian Oldfield;" most were laudatory.

"Well, that's that," said Mallow. "The case now makes absolutely no sense at all. Pyke, pack all these things up and take them with you for fingerprinting."

"What a curious assortment," remarked Edwina. "Isn't that Silas Painter's stick? How did it get here? And the wig and the whiskers and the spectacles — are they some kind of disguise? No — wait a moment — I've got it." She went into the alcove. "There — it's the same outfit as in the print of 'The Virtuous Villain.'"

"Come along, sir," said Pyke to Marjoram. "I'll be taking you back to Fenchester."

"Yes — thank you," said Mallow. "I'm sorry you had to come all this way."

"Not at all, Inspector, not at all," replied Marjoram. He went back to the safe and gently ran his fingers over it. "What a beautiful piece of work it is, to be sure… Goodbye, sir, I wish you luck. Miss — Edwina, is it? A pleasure to meet you. If your father still has plans of this safe, I should be most interested to see them. Just call Scotland Yard and tell them you want to get in touch with Thomas Marjoram." And with a courtly old-fashioned bow he followed Pyke out of the study.

Mallow cleared his throat. "Ahem — Miss Hackett, I wish to thank you for your — um —valuable assistance," he began. "I also —um — wish to apologise for my loss of temper — it was both unprofessional and — er — ungentlemanly."

"And very human," replied Edwina with a smile. "Accepted, of course, Inspector, and no offense taken. I'm sure this case has been a heavy load to bear — and for my part I confess you have been subjected to a fair amount of unnecessary — provocation, shall we say?" She held out her hand. After a moment Mallow took it.

"Excuse me, sir," said Bellman. "We've only just enough time to get to the inquest."

"Oh — right," replied Mallow. "May we drive you down to the village, Miss Hackett?"

"Thank you, I'd appreciate that," said Edwina.

They went out of the study. In the hall they encountered Cabell, Pembert, and William.

"All ready for the inquest?" asked Edwina.

"Just waiting for Muirdyke," replied Cabell.

"Maybe he's still in the billiard room," said Edwina. "I'll go fetch him." She had taken a couple of steps in that direction when Muirdyke came into the hall. Waving a greeting, he cheerfully cried out, "Here we all are! Ready to go to the jolly old inquest, what? Yoicks!" He walked unsteadily toward the door, staggered sideways, and sat down abruptly in an armchair. "Sorry." He looked ruefully at his legs. "They're not behaving very well, dash it."

"Good Lord!" said Edwina. "He's tight."

"As an owl," agreed Cabell.

"What shall we do? We can't let him go like this." Muirdyke was now leaning back in the chair, eyes closed, humming "Five Foot Two, Eyes of Blue."

"Go without him, I suppose, and give an excuse to the coroner."

"No, no, no, no, no," said Muirdyke. Without opening his eyes he gestured vaguely. "You go on ahead. I'll be along in a minute. Just waiting for the old pins to steady up."

"*That* won't do," said Edwina. She went and stood in front of him. "Charles Muirdyke, you are in no shape to go anywhere. Go to bed and sleep it off."

"What, what?" responded Muirdyke. "Maybe you're right." He rose to his feet and sat down again. Pembert and William assisted him to stand, took his arms, and led him carefully to the stairs. Passing Edwina he stopped and looked closely at her. "But they're hazel," he said distinctly. He lurched into motion again and the three men ascended.

Pembert and William returned a few minutes later. "I took the precaution of locking the door," said the butler, "although I doubt he'll be getting up any time soon."

"Good idea," said Mallow. "Does he get drunk often?"

"Not usually as bad as this."

"He's had a hard day," said Edwina. "Shall we go?"

14

IF YOU THINK YOU CAN PUT A NAME TO THE KILLER

The parish hall was already full and the coroner in his chair when the party from Minstrel Manor arrived. Fortunately, Mr. Radford had directed that seats be reserved for the witnesses. There was considerable craning of necks and muted commentary among the villagers, most of whom had never laid eyes on any of them.

"Which one is the inspector, Sarah?" "That one, I think." "He looks quite distinguished, doesn't he?" "No, Sarah, that one's Mr. Cabell. The inspector is the one in spectacles." "Ooh — he's awfully young."

"Stop waving at Higgins — you're embarrassing him. See, he's turned quite red."

"Who's the girl?" "She's staying at the manor. I've heard she paints." "Really? Her face looks ordinary." "Not herself, silly. She paints *pictures.*"

Much of the murmuring concerned Pembert. Mallow's call to Cabell the day before had not gone unnoticed by the Minstrel Folly telephone operator. No one in the village, or on the estate, had seen the inside of a gaol since old Ezekiel Painter, Silas's father, had done ten days for poaching in 1903; so a convicted felon was a sight indeed.

"You wouldn't think it to look at him." "I dunno, he looks shifty to me."

"Do you think he did it?" "What, the murder?" "Of course." "Forgery's not murder."

"Once a crook, always a crook. Bet you a tanner he did it." "Taken."

The church clock sounded four strokes. At the fourth Mr. Radford opened the proceedings by banging a gavel. The buzz of conversation died away, but not soon enough to suit him. He banged it again and, glaring at the onlookers, demanded silence.

The jury, after being selected and sworn, trooped into the next room to view the body. A minute later they returned, some a little green about the gills, and took their places.

"I call Charles Muirdyke," announced Mr. Radford.

Mallow, Cabell, and Edwina looked at each other. After a moment Cabell rose and said, "Mr. Muirdyke is not here, as he is indisposed."

"I can guess why," replied the coroner. "This is most unfortunate. I was counting on him to identify the deceased."

"I can do that. I worked with Mr. Oldfield for many years."

"Very well. Come forward and be sworn."

Cabell viewed the body, testified it was that of Sebastian Oldfield, and went back to his seat.

Mr. Radford then called Dr. Melmoth, who described Mr. Oldfield's injuries.

"In your opinion, then," said the coroner at the conclusion of Dr. Melmoth's testimony, "could the injuries you have described have been accidental or self-inflicted?"

"Certainly not," snorted the doctor.

"I beg your pardon?" said Mr. Radford icily.

"They could not have been either accidental or self-inflicted," said Dr. Melmoth, slowly and distinctly, as to a lackwit. There were titters in the audience. Mr. Radford flushed and banged his gavel. He took a moment to regain his temper before saying, "You may step down, doctor."

Mallow rose and addressed the coroner. "Sir, I request an adjournment while our investigations continue."

"I think not, Inspector," replied Mr. Radford.

Mallow remained on his feet, his mouth agape. He groped for words but found none.

"You may sit down, Inspector," said Mr. Radford. "I call Arthur Pembert."

Pembert took the seat vacated by Dr. Melmoth.

"I understand you are the one who found Mr. Oldfield's body?"

"Yes." The coroner went on to elicit the butler's account of finding Mr. Oldfield dead and calling Constable Higgins to report the murder.

Mallow sat tensed, fidgeting with his spectacles, during the questioning of Pembert, waiting for the butler's past to come up. When it was over he sagged and let out a loud sigh of relief. Mr. Radford gave him a sidelong glance but said nothing.

Edwina leaned across Cabell, who was sitting between her and Mallow. "What's he up to?" she whispered.

"I don't know," whispered Mallow in reply. "Maybe he's just curious."

William was called and testified to seeing Mr. Oldfield alive at seven.

Constable Higgins came next. Taking out his notebook, he related his interviews of Pembert and Edwina.

"In your examination of the study, did you see any signs of a struggle?" asked the coroner.

"No, sir," answered Higgins.

"Thank you. I call Detective-Inspector George Mallow."

Mr. Radford's first question was: "You investigated the scene of the crime?"

"Yes."

"Please describe your investigations."

Mallow went over them. Not wanting to bring up extraneous matters, he said merely he had gone through Oldfield's desk, without describing the contents. He also left out the note, the safe, and the scraps of paper leading to the missing *Panopticon.*

"Could the killer — I think it is safe to say Mr. Oldfield was killed by another — have entered or left the study by the window?" asked Mr. Radford when Mallow was done.

"No. The window was locked, which could only have been done from the inside; it was also obstructed by snow."

"The door into the passage?"

"That is possible."

"The door to the staircase?"

"He could have entered that way, but not left." Mallow described the boxes.

"*Now* what is he up to?" Edwina asked Cabell while Mallow was testifying. "Why does it matter how the killer came and went?"

"He may have seen the story in the *Times* and is trying to confirm whether or not it was a burglar," replied Cabell. "I suppose that's why he asked Higgins if there had been a struggle."

"Then he must have used the door into the passage?" asked Mr. Radford.

"Not necessarily. There was a fourth way: a concealed door opening into the library. However, someone was in the library the entire time from seven, when Mr. Oldfield was last seen alive, until ten, when his body was found."

"Who was this person?"

"Miss Edwina Hackett."

Mr. Radford consulted his list of witnesses. "I see. Thank you. I call Edwina Hackett." Edwina came forward.

"You have heard William Simms state that Mr. Oldfield was alive at seven. Can you confirm this?"

"Yes."

"Did you see him?"

"No, but I heard his voice."

"You have heard Arthur Pembert state that Mr. Oldfield was dead at ten. Can you confirm *this?*"

"Yes."

"Between those two times, did anyone come along the passage toward or away from the study?"

"No one."

"Did anyone come through the library?"

"No."

Mr. Radford's demeanour had been calm and businesslike ever since Dr. Melmoth was dismissed. Now he looked at his notes and frowned. Mallow, watching him, at once recognised his expression of distaste.

"I understand you entered the study shortly after ten?"

"Yes."

"Why?"

"Curiosity."

"*Curiosity?* You were *curious* to view the corpse of a murdered man?"

"Not just that — the scene of the crime. You see —"

"Oh! The 'scene of the crime.' Are you a policewoman?"

"Well, no."

"No. You were just *curious.* Typical behaviour of the younger generation. I see it everywhere. No reverence in the face of death; no respect for authority..." The coroner expressed his opinion of the younger generation at some length, concluding with, "You Bright Young People are all alike: callous, shameless, immodest, interested only in thrills. You should be ashamed of yourself. You may step down."

Edwina, trembling with rage and mortification, stumbled on her way back to her seat and was caught by Mallow. "That *stupid, sanctimonious* —" she hissed.

"Ssh — he'll hear you."

"I don't give a damn. 'Younger generation' indeed! He's not even old enough to be my father —" Edwina was cut short by the repeated banging of Mr. Radford's gavel. She gave him a venomous look, which he returned with interest.

"I call Inspector Mallow again," announced the coroner. Mallow returned to the witness's chair. He saw Mr. Radford's attitude had changed again. The coroner now looked smug and alert, like a cat at a mousehole.

"I take it that in the course of your investigations, Inspector, you looked for fingerprints?"

"We did."

"Why did you not say so earlier?"

"I did not think them relevant to this inquiry."

"You did not think them relevant? Who is conducting this inquest?"

"You are, sir."

"Then *I* will decide what is relevant. Have any been identified as those of a criminal?"

"Yes," said Mallow. "We found the fingerprints of one Alfred Phelps Pemberton."

"A burglar?"

"No."

"What, then?"

"A forger."

"A forger?"

"Yes."

"Have you found any evidence of forgery?"

You're on oath, George. "Yes."

Mr. Radford raised his eyebrows. *He wasn't expecting that,* thought Edwina. *He looks like someone just gave him a Christmas present.*

"What sort of evidence?" asked the coroner.

"There was a paper in Mr. Oldfield's desk on which someone had been practising to copy Mr. Oldfield's signature."

"And you did not think *this* relevant?"

"May I remind you, sir," retorted Mallow with some heat, "that this is an inquiry into murder —not into forgery."

Good for you, George, thought Edwina.

"You need not tell me my job, Inspector," replied Mr. Radford, unruffled.

"If we're going to go into *every* aspect of the police investigation —"

"You may step down, Inspector."

"Damn him," muttered Mallow to Edwina. "I could have hit him with Merryweather, and Callender, and the contents of the safe, and confused him completely. As it is —"

"Arthur Pembert." *Oh, no,* thought Mallow and Edwina simultaneously.

"Yes, sir?"

The cat pounced. "What is your legal name?"

"Alfred Pemberton."

"Why are you calling yourself Arthur Pembert?"

"I — I thought it best —" Pembert paused, swallowed, added "because —" and stopped.

"You thought it best, perhaps, because as Alfred Pemberton you had been convicted of forgery?"

Edwina shot to her feet. "What the *Hell* has this to do with the murder?" she shouted. "Pembert made no secret of his conviction — Mr. Oldfield and Mr. Cabell both knew of it from the start!"

"You will sit down and keep silent, Miss Hackett," snapped Mr. Radford. "The witness will please answer the question."

Pembert had regained his composure. He looked at Mr. Radford and said firmly, "Yes."

"That will be all," said the coroner. He turned and addressed the jury. "Members of the jury, you have heard the testimony of the witnesses.

"The task before you is threefold. Firstly, you must determine, if possible, *how* Sebastian Oldfield met his death. The evidence on this point is quite clear: Dr. Melmoth has testified that Mr. Oldfield died as the result of several blows to the head.

"Secondly, you must determine, if possible, whether Mr. Oldfield's death was accident, suicide, or murder. The evidence on this point is also clear: it could not have been accident or suicide.

"Thirdly, if possible, you must determine the identity of the person who did the foul deed. From several witnesses you have heard that Mr. Oldfield was alive at seven o'clock in the evening and dead at ten. You have heard that entry to the study was impossible save through the passage or the staircase. You have heard that exit *from* the study was impossible save through the passage. You have heard that no one came through the passage between seven o'clock and ten, save Alfred Pemberton. It is your duty to determine that Mr. Oldfield was killed by some other person or persons. If you think you can put a name to the killer or killers, it is your duty to do so. You may retire and consider your verdict."

The jury did not retire. They huddled together for a brief whispered conference. At its conclusion, the foreman stepped forward and announced their verdict: Sebastian Oldfield had been murdered by Alfred Pemberton, alias Arthur Pembert.

Edwina was on her feet again. "Pembert *couldn't* have done the murder," she cried. "Mr. Oldfield was dead long before —"

"You will sit down and be silent, Miss Hackett," commanded Mr. Radford. "This inquest is concluded."

15

I ARREST YOU ON THE CHARGE OF KILLING SEBASTIAN OLDFIELD

The hall filled with babble. The spectators crowded toward the main door, eager to reassemble at the Green Wyvern and discuss the proceedings they had just seen and heard. Reporters from the Fenchester *Times* and the Chiltonbury *Intelligencer* looked about vainly for Mr. Radford, who had made a quick exit. They turned on Mallow and Pembert. Seeing the Press coming, notebooks at the ready, Mallow herded the stunned butler and the other witnesses into the room where the corpse of Oldfield lay, closed the door, and leaned against it. Bellman joined him. After the first jar from the pressmen outside, the sergeant shouted through the door that they were committing assault against officers of the police. The attempt to force the door ceased. The quicker-witted of the two crouched and put his ear to the keyhole.

"That *idiot!*" blazed Edwina. "That thick-headed disgrace! Who made him a coroner?"

"I believe —" began Cabell but Edwina rode over him. "Whoever it was, I'll be on his doorstep first thing tomorrow!"

"Quite right," agreed Dr. Melmoth. "The man's an ass."

Cabell noticed the door could be latched from their side. He did so and Mallow and Bellman stepped away. Edwina went and stood by the white and trembling Pembert. "What are we going to *do?*" she asked.

"I'm afraid, Miss Hackett, we're going to do our duty," said Mallow. He nodded to Bellman, who advanced to Pembert and put a hand on the butler's shoulder. "Alfred Pemberton, alias Arthur Pembert, I arrest you on the charge of killing Sebastian Oldfield; and I warn you anything you say shall be taken down and may be used in evidence."

"Are you *another* idiot?" cried Edwina. Heedless of the fact that *she* was committing assault on an officer of the law, she thrust herself between Pembert and Bellman and tried to push the latter's arm away. "Why not arrest *me?* There's just as much against me as against Pembert — you said so yourself!"

"Miss Hackett," said Mallow. "among ourselves, I agree with you. What happened out there was a gross miscarriage. But the fact remains that the verdict was against Pembert. I have no choice but to arrest him."

"But you'll keep looking until you find the real murderer?" asked Edwina.

"That will be up to the Superintendent," replied Mallow.

"Then I'll be on *his* doorstep first thing tomorrow morning."

"You needn't bother. I shall put the case to him quite as strongly as you could."

A second door in the room led to the outside. Mallow put his finger to his lips and pointed to it. The others took the hint and made a quiet exit. When they were gone, he gently unlatched the door by which he stood and yanked it open. The two eavesdroppers on the other side tumbled in.

"Nothing you may have overheard is for the record," Mallow told them. "Print one word and we'll be down on you like a ton of bricks. Except you may say Pembert has been arrested."

"Won't you give us *something?*" asked the reporter from the *Intelligencer.*

Mallow indicated the body. "You may interview Mr. Oldfield —

I've no objection to that." He left through the second door. Darkness had come during the inquest. It was a few moments before he could make out Pembert, standing between Higgins and Bellman. Edwina remained nearby.

"We'll have to take Pembert back to Fenchester, Miss Hackett," said Mallow. "Can I drive you and Mr. Cabell and William up to the manor first?"

"No, thank you, I'll walk," replied Edwina. "Mr. Cabell has left already. William said Cabell or no Cabell, he was going to the Wyvern."

A bitter wind was blowing through Minstrel Folly and Mallow felt the sting of snow on his face. "Are you sure you don't want a lift?"

"I need to let off some steam. Walking will be good for me."

"Very well. Oh — before I forget." He fumbled in his pocket and took out Pembert's and Cabell's keys to the study. "I was going to give these back." He handed them to Edwina. "One of these is Mr. Cabell's. Could you please return it to him?"

"I will." Edwina turned to Pembert. "Don't worry. I'll come and see you tomorrow."

The walk back to Minstrel Manor was not enough to calm Edwina. She had no one to talk to — Cabell had retired to the workshop and Muirdyke was asleep. She sat down to work on Oldfield's portrait but could not get even as far as picking up a tube of paint. Instead she took up a sketching block and a pencil and drew caricatures of Mr. Radford, each ruder than the last; then tore them all to shreds. *War and Peace* she put aside after only a page. Finally she went into the hall to write a new letter to Dorothy Mowbray.

Dear Dot,
    Where to begin?

Just got back from the inquest, where a blithering FOOL of a coroner stage-managed a verdict against the butler. He couldn't have been more obvious if he'd started building a gallows! The Inspector had to arrest him (the butler, that is, not the coroner — unfortunately, aggravated stupidity with intent to spout hogwash is not a crime), but hopes he'll be allowed to continue the investigation. If he isn't, then I will. Just like in the books, where the plucky young heroine and hero show up the police (although in this case it's not their fault). And I could have, too, if I'd thought of it in time, but I got slapped down.

You mayn't believe it, but the plucky young heroine could have had a choice of heroes. Earlier today Mr. Cabell and Mr. Muirdyke proposed! Or tried to — I managed to choke them both off before either one said anything definite. I never knew my brain could work that fast. I daresay I'll get married someday, but not anytime soon — and I'd like to get to know the man a little better first.

I managed to tick off the Inspector again — twice — but the second time wasn't really my fault and he apologised. He is quite a gentleman, and perhaps we'll be friends before the case is over. That might be a while — there seem to be a couple of mysterious figures involved, a Barnabas Merryweather (who's really a character in a play, but someone's going about dressed up as him), and a Robert Callender, who killed his wife years ago and may or may not be dead.

It occurs to me that if poor Pembert (that's the butler) hadn't happened to have a prison record, it could just as well be me in gaol! I was on the spot and could have killed Mr. Oldfield just as easily. It may come to murder yet, if I run across that coroner on a dark night with no one about...

I must stop here — I have to see about putting some things together to take to Pembert tomorrow (I don't know what — I suppose I'll ring up the Inspector and ask what people in gaol need). Why is it up to me, you ask? Mr. Cabell is in his workshop again — all he ever does is work — and Mr. Muirdyke is sleeping it off after getting thoroughly squiffed today.

Hugs,

Edie

P.S. The blockhead had the effrontery to call me a Bright Young Person!

As if I'd get within a hundred yards of any *of those gin-soaked, promiscuous drug addicts! Except Rodney, but he's not too far gone — is he? If he is, give him the push even if it hurts. E.*

Mallow refused to discuss the case during the return to Fenchester. "I don't even want to *think* about this investigation until I've had some coffee," he said to Bellman. "It's not Doyle, and it's not Dickens — it's Alice in bloody Wonderland. When we get back, make a pot — *strong*. If Henley and the others who are out looking for Merry-weather —" Mallow let out a sardonic bark of laughter "— are back, send them to my office. Leave everything we found in the safe there. I'll be reporting to the Superintendent. And what am I going to say to him?"

Runciman said not a word while Mallow poured out his tale of woe, only uttering a soft "tsk-tsk" from time to time. "George, George," he said when Mallow was done. "You blotted your copybook there."

"*I* did, sir?" replied Mallow in surprise.

"If Pembert *were* guilty — but, like you, I don't think he is — it would be difficult to convict him; or if he were convicted, the verdict would certainly be reversed on appeal; and the court would make you look pretty silly. You didn't give him a caution before the inquest, and you didn't advise him that he should have legal representation."

"I had no idea the coroner was going to do what he did."

"You should have spoken with Radford ahead of time and settled on an adjournment; or told him there were other suspects and asked for a directed verdict against persons unknown."

"There wasn't time —"

"What about when you met with him yesterday morning?"

"Oh — of course, sir."

"And you needn't have had all those witnesses. It was an open invitation to Radford to call them."

"Yes, sir."

"That said, Radford *is* a B.F., and so was his father before him." Runciman paused, then went on, "In fairness to him, this was his first inquest into a murder. It seems to have gone to his head. Still, I'll have a word with one or two of the county councillors — or perhaps talk with Radford first. He may not be totally impervious to sense. As for you, George, go to your office, let your hair down, and have a good cry. Then get back on the case. You've found out a remarkable amount in three days — no wonder you're feeling overwhelmed. Now it's time to sit and think."

"Yes, sir."

Porlock, Henley, and Vanderleun were waiting in his office when Mallow returned. He walked past them without acknowledging their presence and sat down at his desk. He decided to forgo the cry; instead he closed his eyes, and tried to think of nothing at all. It didn't work. As unwanted memories will do, his outburst at Edwina came back to him again and again. *God, how embarrassing — in front of Bellman and Marjoram too. Edwina — that is, Miss Hackett — took it kindly enough. Why did I say "Edwina"?*

Pyke entered, followed by Bellman with the coffee. Without opening his eyes, Mallow stretched out his arm for a cup. The others waited patiently while he slowly sipped it. When it was done he opened his eyes, handed the cup back to Bellman for a refill, and said, "All right. Where are we?"

"I'm sorry, sir," said Henley. "We couldn't find Merryweather anywhere. Have you heard anything from Chiltonbury?"

"No," replied Mallow. "We can call off the search. Merryweather has been found — and he's dead." He and Bellman grinned at the expressions of the others.

"What, sir?" said Porlock.

"Sebastian Oldfield and Barnabas Merryweather are — or were — one and the same. Once upon a time, Oldfield was an actor, and Merryweather was a character he played. We found the costume in Oldfield's safe — right down to the wig. For some reason, which I can't even begin to guess, Oldfield dressed himself up, opened an account in Chiltonbury, and paid himself six thousand pounds. That reminds me — Henley?" Mallow took out the copy of the letter to Maunder & Co. "Compare that with the cheques we found in the safe. There they are."

Henley looked at the letter and the cheques. "The signatures match, all right. But — excuse me for a moment." He left the office, coming back a little later with the cheques from the workshop and the papers found in Oldfield's desk. After studying them for a minute or so, he said, "Yes. The signature on the cheques to Merryweather is a pretty good copy of that on the others, and matches the one on the papers. But —"

"But what?" asked Mallow.

"If Oldfield wrote the letter, you'd expect the handwriting to match the signature. But in fact the handwriting matches *Merryweather's* signature. I can understand he might want two different handwritings for two different identities... But no. Even a disguised hand has points of similarity with the same individual's normal hand. These are completely different."

"Well, of course they are," said Bellman. "Pembert wrote the letter, at Oldfield's request."

"He *said*, at Oldfield's request," said Mallow.

"So *Pembert* is Merryweather?" asked Porlock. "But you said, sir, it was Oldfield."

"So I did," replied Mallow. "Maybe I was wrong. Maybe he and Pembert took it in turns. Maybe he, and Pembert, and Cabell, and Muirdyke, and Painter, and Miss Hackett *all* took it in turns. Is there any more coffee? Thanks." His eyes fell on Merryweather's blue coat.

"Let's see…" he mused. He looked at each of the others. "Vanderleun, you're closest to Oldfield's build. Try on that coat."

Vanderleun did so.

"Fits you to a T. That rules out Pembert, who's much shorter than you, and Cabell, who's much taller. Neither could wear it without looking absurd. Besides, both of them are thinner — so is Muirdyke."

"If Oldfield knew about — what Sergeant Henley said about a disguised hand," put in Pyke, "he'd have wanted to copy someone else's to use as Merryweather, and there was Pembert's all ready for him. But still, why do it in the first place?"

Henley held up the papers from Oldfield's desk. "And say *this* was Oldfield practising Merryweather's signature," he said, waving the paper in his left hand, "what about *that?*" He waved the other one. "Why would Oldfield have to practise his *own* signature?"

Mallow's telephone rang. He picked it up. "Sergeant Guntram here, sir. There's a message from the Chiltonbury force. They were looking for a Barnabas Merryweather, at our request, and they've got a line on him. From time to time he took a room at a hotel. The hotel was reluctant to let him stay at first, because he wanted the room for only a couple of hours, but he convinced them it wasn't for immoral purposes."

"Of course not," said Mallow. "Thank you, Guntram." He hung up. "Confirmation of a sort. We know — or can make a pretty good guess — what Oldfield was doing when Pembert drove him into Chiltonbury. He was changing himself into Merryweather to go to the bank."

"I have another question," spoke up Porlock, who had been studying the playbills and clippings. "Oldfield was acting pretty continuously from 1894 to 1912. How old was he?"

"Fifty," said Bellman.

"Then he was born in 1877, which means he started acting when he was 16 or 17. Between learning his lines, rehearsing, and performing — when did he find time to get all his technical knowledge?"

"Cabell said he only had to read something once," said Mallow. "He could get through a lot of books in eighteen years. He'd learn his lines quickly, too."

"And he started out in small parts," added Pyke. "Look at the early playbills. In *Richard III* he's Catesby. In *Captured by Pirates* he's Spargett, the First Mate. And so on.

"Yes," said Mallow. "And, don't forget, he acted in repertory. They'd have a stock set of plays and do them over and over."

"All this is very well," spoke up Vanderleun. "But do we *know* this whole Merryweather business has anything to do with the murder?"

"We don't," admitted Mallow. "But we don't know it doesn't, so we have to dig until we do know one way or the other. The same with Callender. Apart from those, we don't have much to go on at all."

"What did Sherlock Holmes say?" put in Bellman. "When you've removed everything that's impossible, whatever remains, no matter how improbable, must be the truth."

"Well then," said Mallow. "What's impossible, so that we may remove it?"

No one spoke. Porlock, seeing the coffeepot empty, took it out to make a fresh one.

"Cabell was on the train to London when the murder was committed," said Vanderleun finally. "I talked to the stationmaster today. He reached the station just before the train left."

"That's one," said Mallow. "Anything else?"

"Oldfield didn't write the note we found," said Henley.

"That's two —" Mallow stopped. "Where's the note?" He rummaged in the pile of evidence on his desk. "Got it!" He looked at the note. Then he took off his spectacles, sat back, and gazed at the ceiling, his eyes unfocused. *It's an absurd idea, and yet...* Before he could dismiss it, the idea set itself down at the center of the puzzle and the other pieces began to arrange themselves about it, neatly coming together to form a picture.

Porlock returned. Henley gestured at him to keep silent.

Without moving, Mallow began to speak. Slowly and exactly, but unable to keep excitement out of his voice, he described how the pieces of the puzzle could be made to fit together. At the end he said, "Now — knock holes in it. It's completely outlandish, and yet it works — so well I'm afraid of it."

The others contemplated Mallow's account. Bellman walked to the window and looked out at the snowflakes swirling in the twilight. Porlock whistled softly. Pyke drummed his fingers on the desk. Henley took out his notebook and doodled. Vanderleun closed his eyes.

At length Bellman turned back to Mallow and said, "It's a remarkable story, sir, and it hangs together wonderfully. But as it stands, it's pure conjecture. How do we find something solid to back it up?"

"Mostly in London," replied Mallow. "You and I will go there tomorrow and hope we can track down someone who remembers Oldfield from the repertory company. We'll also pay a call on the Yard and look at the Callender file. Pyke will come with us. Henley — tomorrow morning, take one of the Merryweather cheques and one of the others and pay a visit to Mr. Radford. I want you to compare the signatures with that on Oldfield's will. Porlock, you and Vanderleun will stay here on call."

16

TRAPPED IN THE STUDY

To her surprise, Edwina slept soundly that night. In the morning she remembered her duty to Pembert and rang up police headquarters in Fenchester.

"East Fenshire police," came the voice of Sergeant Daw.

"This is Edwina Hackett, calling from Minstrel Manor. You have a prisoner in your gaol — Arthur Pembert. May I speak to him?"

"Are you his solicitor?"

"No — just a friend. I want to know if I can bring him anything."

"We'll ask him and let you know."

"Very well. Is Inspector Mallow there? I need to speak to him also. I have important evidence regarding the murder of Sebastian Oldfield."

"The inspector has gone to London, Miss Hackett. He is expected to return later in the day. Shall I see if there is anyone here who can take your evidence?"

"No. I'll wait for the inspector to return."

Some time later Daw returned her call. Pembert had asked for a toothbrush, a comb, a change of clothes, and his Bible. With William's assistance she packed a small suitcase with these articles and set out.

Snow was falling lightly but the roads were passable. At the gaol Edwina delivered the suitcase and asked to see Pembert. She was taken to a small room furnished with a table and two chairs and told to wait. After a time Pembert was escorted in, his appearance shockingly altered overnight: grey and shrunken, he shuffled rather than walked. "Good Lord, Pembert, you look *awful,*" cried Edwina, and at once wished the words unsaid.

"Thank you for coming," replied Pembert in a weak and quavering voice. "This is very kind of you… Ever since I came out of prison I've had nightmares that I was back inside. Now it's a living nightmare and I can't wake up."

"Buck up, Pembert," said Edwina. "Never say die. You have friends who are working for you. There's me, for one, and Mr. Muirdyke —" *Not strictly true, since he's still asleep and knows nothing of your plight; but I'm sure whose side he'll come down on.* "— And the inspector is on the trail of the real murderer. You'll be out in no time."

"I wish I could believe you. But I can't see beyond the walls and the bars."

"None of that. All will be well… I suppose the next thing to do is get you a lawyer. Mr. Oldfield's solicitor would be the one to apply to. Who is he?"

Pembert emitted a surprising bark of laughter. "Henry Radford."

"The clown of yesterday's pantomime? That *would* be a joke. First he puts you in here, then he's tasked with getting you out? I *don't* think. We'll see about getting you someone *competent.*" A knock sounded on the door. "Our time's up. Goodbye — I'll see you back at the manor."

"Please remember to ask for the key to Mr. Charles's bedroom on your way out."

Driving back to the manor through a light but steady snow, Edwina fell prey to doubts. *It's all very well to talk about working for Pembert, but*

what can one actually do? *Charles is still in bed — probably with a headache, which would serve him right — and Cabell is in the workshop as usual... I suppose I can at least get the portrait out of the way.*

At the manor she found a scene of consternation. Muirdyke was awake, trapped in his room, and threatening to break down the door with a poker; the servants were running about looking for a key. Edwina went up and unlocked the door. It was at once opened, revealing Muirdyke barefoot and clad in green-and-yellow striped pyjamas. "What the devil is going on?" he exclaimed. "Where's Pembert? Why — oh, dash it." He closed the door and a few moments later opened it again, now decent in slippers and a dressing-gown. "Er — good morning," he said.

"Good morning," replied Edwina. There was no friendship in her voice. "To answer your questions: we had to lock you in your bedroom to prevent you making yourself look an idiot at the inquest. Pembert has been arrested for murdering your uncle and is at the gaol in Fenchester; if you can think of anything to do for him, I suggest you do it. I'm going to the library to work and I would prefer not to be disturbed."

Suiting her actions to her words, Edwina went down to her studio, sat down at her easel, and worked steadily through the afternoon. At one point Muirdyke looked in, intending to suggest a walk down to the Wyvern, but wisely changed his mind.

Mallow and Bellman returned to headquarters at about six-thirty, tired but cheerful and even excited. They had learned, not only was the Holborn Repertory Company still going, but the current manager had been the assistant manager when "S. Oldfield" was performing. He had proved to be a mine of information. The Callender file had turned out to be another rich lode. They had boarded the train to Fenchester at the end of the day with Mallow's conjectures firmly grounded in fact.

Henley was waiting for them. "You were quite correct, sir," he said to Mallow. "Oldfield's signature on the will was nothing like the signatures on the cheques. Mr. Radford was mightily put out to learn we were still investigating. He was convinced he'd solved the case himself."

"Henry Radford can stand on his head and whistle 'Dixie.' We'll drive to Minstrel Manor and make the arrest at once," said Mallow.

"In this weather, sir?" asked Bellman.

"The murderer may bolt at any time. We've no time to lose." *Besides, this is my big case, I've cracked it, and I want to wrap it up at once.*

The snow which had been falling off and on since the day before had been merely an outrider for the ferocious storm now roaring over Fenshire. Now, blown and drifted by the blustering wind, it made the roads even worse than they had been on Mallow's first journey to the Manor. "I doubt we'll get there before nine o'clock," said Bellman as they exited Fenchester at ten miles an hour.

"As long as we get there," replied Mallow.

At a quarter to seven Edwina set down her brush and contemplated the portrait of Sebastian Oldfield. *What is it they say? "The supreme gift of an artist is knowing when to stop." I guess it's time. But now what? Wait for news from the inspector? Write to Dot? Go with Charles to the Wyvern? (Ten to one he's there already.) No, I must do something to help Pembert. Maybe if I were to look in the study again?* She given Cabell his key back that morning, but the other was still in the pocket of her coat. She fetched it and opened the study door, turning the key clockwise.

But where to begin? Look for *another* concealed door? Barring trapdoors in the ceiling or under the carpet, the obvious place was the wall behind the model railway. Edwina called up a mental picture of Sebastian Oldfield sitting calmly at his desk as a sinister figure opened a secret door and clambered over the trains. *I'm afraid that's really rather silly. Under the table is the place to look.*

Behind her came a hiss as the door into the passage closed.

It took Edwina a moment to realise she was trapped in the study. Then she was seized with panic. She looked wildly about for a way out. She ran to the French window and tried it. The window was locked. As if in mockery, a mass of snow fell from the roof and blocked the window.

The door in the alcove? She tried it and it opened. She ran up the stairs — and found the door at the top locked.

Of course — the door into the library. Edwina found the button, pushed it, put her hand on the door — and remembered the just-completed portrait on the other side, the paint still wet; and on the table beside it, the jar of turps with her brushes in it.

Gingerly she pulled her hand back. *Pull yourself together, Edwina. Running around gormlessly won't get you anywhere. Have to think. Or at least distract yourself.* She looked about. The desk was still a mess. *Why hasn't the study been cleaned? Of course — it's been locked and sealed.*

Edwina had seen Oldfield's cleaning materials on the shelves by the foot of the stairs. She fetched them and set to work, tipping the remnants of food into the wastepaper basket, giving the dishes and utensils a wipe, and mopping up the butter. It had run over the edge of the desk and dripped on to the carpet. She returned to the shelves and found a bottle of benzine.

Wait a minute. She stood still, the bottle in her hand. *The butter hadn't run that far on the night of the murder. And when I saw it then, it was congealed.* She tried to remember what the desk had looked like when she was in the study the previous afternoon. *No — it was close to the edge, but hadn't run over... Oh, of course — the sun shines in during the day... No, it doesn't. The window faces northeast. And the weather's been cloudy since Tuesday. Something strange is going on.*

Cleaning done, Edwina sat down in the armchair for a rest. The bound *Panopticon* lay on the table beside her; she took it up, hoping it would provide a new distraction. Seeing it was the volume for 1926 she turned at once to the August issue, hoping to find a clue there with a closer reading.

*What's this? The issue has been torn out... Did the inspector do it? No —
the copy in his office was intact. So he went to the trouble of getting a back
issue. And then he asked about Robert Callender, so there must be some
connection. What was in the story? Can't remember much, except the picture.
An interesting face.*

~

"So far, so good," said Mallow. They had reached the outskirts of
Swannington.

"There's one good thing anyhow," remarked Bellman. "If the
murderer does bolt, he won't get away very fast in this stuff."

"Quite. Careful, Pyke — you almost had us in the ditch there."

"Sorry, sir," replied Pyke. "It's hard to see the road."

~

A fresh ripple of panic ran through Edwina. She put the book down,
closed her eyes, and began to imagine: *I'm in a vast meadow; I'm at the
seashore, looking out over the waves at the distant horizon; I'm in the middle
of the Sahara Desert.* She felt a current of warm air waft about her legs.
That's some imagination, Edwina. The current grew stronger and she
realised she wasn't imagining it.

Opening her eyes, Edwina looked about. The air was coming from
one of several louvers in the base of the wall. She grew conscious of a
faint rumble below and a vibration in the floor. *Central heating's
come on.*

The rumble grew louder, the current stronger, and the air hotter.
All right, I know it's winter outside, but you can stop now. Hotter still;
uncomfortably hot; and Edwina's panic returned. *Am I going to be
roasted alive?* She retreated up the stairs and pounded on the door
and cried out, but no one came. The heat followed her up and she
realised the only thing worse than being stuck in the study was
being stuck at the end of a narrow cul-de-sac. She descended and

looked wildly about. *The window! Even if I can't get out I can get some cool air.*

Edwina took up the *Panopticon,* went to the window, and struck a pane. Being made of Oldfield's Unbreakable Glass, it did not even crack. She struck it again and again, with no effect. She turned to the desk, looking for something harder or heavier than the book and saw the telephone.

Charles Muirdyke walked out of the Wyvern and into the storm. "Dash it all!" he said to himself. "It wasn't like this when I came here." Lowering his head, he pulled his coat-collar close about his face and began to trudge back to Minstrel Manor.

Edwina lay down the book, snatched up the telephone and pushed a button at random. The telephone at the other end rang and rang but no one answered. She tried again and at the second ring a voice said "Yes?"

"Who is this?" asked Edwina, her voice almost a scream.

"Cabell."

"I'm in the study and the door closed on me and all the other doors are locked and I'm stuck. Come and get me OUT!"

"No need for that. Do you see the row of buttons on the desk? Push the first one."

Edwina pushed the button and the door opened. With a gasp of relief she fled into the passage and took deep breaths of the cooler air, until a billow of heat from the study engulfed her. She went back in and picked up the telephone. "Are you still there, Mr. Cabell?"

"Yes."

"Something's gone terribly wrong with the central heating. The study's like an oven."

Silence.

"Mr. Cabell?"

"I'll be right there."

Edwina retreated farther down the passage, away from the heat. Before long Cabell arrived at a run, wearing an overcoat dusted with snow. He hurried into the study. Edwina followed him, curious to see what he would do.

Cabell pushed another button and the clock and thermometer appeared, the pointer of the latter at 100 degrees. He turned the knob beneath it and the pointer moved lower. When it reached fifty he pushed the knob. "Damned system's *still* not working right," he explained. "Problems ever since it was installed."

The rumble below stopped, then resumed in a different key. A chilly breeze from the louvers eddied about Edwina's ankles.

"Thank you, Mr. Cabell — I thought I was in an oven. A minute later and you'd have found me done to a turn."

"I'm very glad I could help. Perhaps it would be best to leave now." Cabell went to the door. Edwina lingered behind, fascinated by the buttons. *So if all they do is control this and that about the study, surely they can't be dangerous.* She pushed one.

The French window slid sideways. The temperature in the study dropped abruptly as it filled with the roar and chill of the winter storm outside.

Edwina stared at the opening. "So the murderer *could* have got in and out by the window!" she exclaimed. "Is the inspector back yet? I have to tell him." She turned to Cabell. "How can I call outside..." Her voice died away as she realised she was looking at the muzzle of a revolver.

Muirdyke, ploughing through the storm, looked up briefly to see how much distance remained between the manor and himself. With relief he saw it was not that far off. Then he looked again. The lights were on in the study and — where was the window? The was only an opening in the wall where the window had been. He changed course and began to walk in that direction.

"Why did you do that, Miss Hackett?" asked Cabell. His voice was soft — and ice-cold.

"I —" For once in her life Edwina found herself at a loss for words.

"I am really *most* terribly sorry, Miss Hackett. Please do not move or cry out." He reached behind him and removed the key. A moment later the door into the passage hissed shut.

Edwina recovered her poise. "I suppose you killed Mr. Oldfield?"

"Between you and me and these four walls — yes."

"Why? And how? You were on the train when he was killed."

"Never mind. This is no time for explanations."

"Then what is this the time for?"

"To decide your fate," replied Cabell. "I should prefer not to have to shoot you, Miss Hackett — I have a great regard for you. Perhaps we can come to an accommodation."

"You really think so?"

"Certainly."

"May I sit down?"

"Of course."

Edwina sat behind the desk. *Now I'm closer to the window than he is, and the desk is between us. If I can distract him...* Edwina edged one hand toward the bound *Panopticon.*

"Don't," said Cabell. "You wouldn't get far. I can move through the snow much faster than you."

"Oh, all right. I suppose there's more to this than I know?" she asked.

"Of course there is — more than you can imagine. But can you be content with what you do know and go away, without speaking of it to anyone — with, shall we say, a double fee for your work?"

"Giving me sixpence again?" Edwina raised her eyes from the revolver to Cabell's face. One eyebrow was raised as he waited for her answer. More snow slid from the roof and spilled into the study, but she didn't hear it. *I've seen that look before...* In her mind's eye — the eye of a portrait painter — she altered the contours of Cabell's face, filled them out. *"Good Lord — you're Robert Callender!"*

Cabell's face paled. He raised the revolver and put his finger on the trigger. Edwina shut her eyes and breathed a brief prayer. A few moments later, finding herself still alive, she opened them again. Cabell had mastered himself.

"Now, how did you know that?" he asked.

"The picture in the *Panopticon.* You had exactly the same look just now. And I remembered you from the workshop — when you were stouter."

Cabell laughed. "And I thought I was so clever. I didn't want a photographer for fear I should accidentally appear in one of his shots — and instead I got *you.* But how did you see my picture? I tore it out."

"The inspector got another copy. I read it in his office. And I don't forget faces."

"Indeed. But let us return to the matter at hand. My offer still stands. Double your fee — or treble — or whatever you want."

Edwina laughed in derision. "Don't be silly. If I were the sort of person who would take an offer like that, I'd take it and then shop you the first chance I got."

"I thought as much; but the attempt had to be made... We are at an impasse."

"Why don't you tell me why you killed Mr. Oldfield?"

"Curiosity? Or playing for time? It won't work. No one can hear us and I have the key."

"There *may* be extenuating circumstances that we can work with. But if we're going to talk, may I close the window? I don't like freezing any more than I like roasting."

"I'll close it. Please keep absolutely still." Cabell, keeping the revolver pointed at Edwina, approached the desk. He pressed the button that controlled the window, which slid six inches and stopped, blocked by the fallen snow. "No matter. We can continue this conversation in the workshop. Come along."

"I'm not dressed for the weather out there — may I borrow your coat?"

"Uh-oh!" cried Pyke. Taking the turn into Minstrel Folly just a little too fast, he felt the car sliding sideways. With a lurch it went off the edge of the road.

"Damn!" exclaimed Mallow. "Almost there! Didn't I tell you to be careful, Pyke?"

"I'm sure I'm very sorry, sir," replied the crestfallen constable.

"What do we do now?" asked Bellman. "Walk up to the manor? Or get some people from the village to come help us get back on to the road?"

"Let's see if we can manage ourselves," said Mallow. "Pyke, Bellman and I will push the car from the front. At my signal, *gently* reverse."

"Yes, sir."

Mallow and Bellman got out, plodded through the snow, and positioned themselves. Mallow signaled to Pyke; then he and the sergeant leaned forward and pushed.

Cabell managed to shrug his left arm out of his overcoat, quickly transferred the revolver to his left hand, and shook the coat off his right arm. The overcoat fell to the floor and he backed away from it. Edwina picked up the coat and put it on. Cabell took firm hold of one of her arms and led her outside. As soon as they were through the window, Edwina let herself go limp and sagged to the ground. Taken by surprise, Cabell loosened his hold. Edwina slipped out of the coat and attempted to scramble to her feet and run. She floundered a few paces through the deep snow and fell headlong.

This mishap saved her life, for Cabell impulsively fired at her just as she fell and the bullet passed over her.

As Cabell moved after Edwina, a shadowy figure launched itself out of the darkness and swirling snow and grappled with him. Cabell fought back desperately. He had held on to the revolver. Using it as a club, he tried to get in a blow on his adversary's head, but was held too closely to strike effectively. Writhing and twisting, he managed to get the gun between himself and the other, and pulled the trigger.

The shot told and the other grunted in shock and let go, but did not retreat. Instead, he let loose a wild haymaker that landed directly on Cabell's jaw. Cabell, dazed, staggered and fell.

～

"Are you all right, sir?" asked Bellman.

"Yes," replied Mallow. His feet had slipped from under him as he pushed, precipitating him face-first into the snow. "Help me up and we'll try again."

They tried again. This time Bellman slipped and fell.

"Third time lucky, they say," encouraged Mallow. "Otherwise we'll walk the rest of the way. Now, *push!*"

The car rocked forwards and backwards as Pyke took his foot on and off the accelerator. Mallow and Bellman timed their efforts to the rhythm of the rocking. The car began to move and slowly backed on to the road.

"Ha!" cried Mallow in triumph. "Let's get going."

～

"Edwina — are you all right?" came a hoarse voice. "It's me — Charles."

Edwina rolled over and looked up. In the light from the study she saw Muirdyke, clutching his left arm with his right hand and standing beside the prone figure of Cabell moving feebly in the snow.

"I'm fine," she gasped. "Charles — you're hurt!"

"Yes, well, that's not important right now. Thank Heaven, *you're* not hurt… We have to do something with this blighter."

"Where is his gun?"

"He must have dropped it when I hit him… Dash this snow — wait, here it is — I have it."

"Give it to me." Muirdyke handed the revolver to Edwina, who continued, "We'll need help. I'll keep an eye on Cabell. You go inside and get William."

Muirdyke entered the study. Edwina backed a few feet away from Cabell and pointed the revolver steadily at him. By this time Cabell had somewhat recovered and was sitting up in the snow, groaning and feeling his jaw. He looked up at Edwina and said rather shakily, "What just happened?"

"I'm sure you'll be able to figure that out for yourself," said Edwina. "Meanwhile, stay where you are." Cabell's eyes focused on the revolver. He nodded and did not move. Inside the study, Muirdyke was on the telephone instructing William to come to the study at once with a first-aid kit, some rope, a bottle of brandy, and a glass — no, two glasses.

A short while later there came a pounding at the study door. "What do I do?" shouted Muirdyke through the window.

"On the desk — the first button," Edwina shouted back. Muirdyke pressed the button and William rushed in.

"All right, Mr. Cabell, you may get up," said Edwina. "Go back into the study."

Cabell clambered to his feet, and stumbled back through the window. Edwina followed, not too closely. "Sit down in the armchair," she said, her voice firm. Cabell obeyed. "You asked for an accommodation earlier? Here it is: you don't move, and I don't shoot you. William, help Mr. Charles out of his overcoat and see to his arm."

Muirdyke grimaced in pain as William eased him out of his overcoat. When the footman saw the blood soaking the sleeve of his suit he turned green and rushed outside. Through the storm came the sound of retching. Muirdyke retrieved a handkerchief from a pocket and managed to wrap it around his arm.

William returned, pale and shaken. "I'm very sorry, Miss 'ackett," he said.

"Never mind," replied Edwina. "Take the rope and tie Mr. Cabell to the chair."

William stood gaping. "Do as Miss Hackett says," ordered Muirdyke.

"Do you know First Aid?" asked Muirdyke while William was securing Cabell.

"I'm afraid not," replied Edwina.

"All right. Take off my tie and use it for a tourniquet, and then bind the handkerchief more tightly about my arm. We'll need scissors to cut off the sleeves. William, go and fetch a pair."

Having seen to Muirdyke's arm, Edwina poured brandy into the glasses and gave one to him. He emptied it in a single gulp. Edwina took a good swallow of her own, for her nerves had been sorely tried and she was now feeling the reaction.

"I say, Edwina — Miss Hackett —" began Muirdyke.

"I think we're on a first-name basis now," replied Edwina. "Thank you, Charles, for saving my life."

"Oh — er — right," replied Charles, gesturing awkwardly with his right hand. "This is a dashed rum business. What's it all about?"

"Cabell killed your uncle," replied Edwina.

"Did he, by Jove?"

William returned with the scissors. Edwina tried to cut off Charles's coat sleeve but the tweed was too tough for her. "William, you'll have to do it… Oh, for God's sake, close your eyes. I'll guide you."

Eventually Charles's arm was bared. Edwina busied herself cleaning and bandaging his wound. The bullet had passed through the left arm above the elbow, fortunately without hitting the bone or a major blood vessel.

"I think I need another brandy," said Charles. Edwina poured it for him. This time he only swallowed half. He looked at Cabell. "So you killed Uncle Sebastian, eh? *Ho, miscreant! You rushed to villainy faster than the hare; but Justice, although slow like the tortoise, has triumphed! Your days of evildoing are ended!*" Edwina and Cabell both gave him a puzzled look. "It's Uncle Sebastian's favourite line from *The Virtuous Villain.* Dashed appropriate, what? I just wish *he* were here — but wherever he is, he's saying it too."

From down the passage came the sound of someone knocking at the front door. Charles nodded at William to go answer it.

Opening the door revealed Inspector Mallow and Sergeant Bellman, barely recognisable under thick coatings of snow. With them was Constable Pyke. "Good evening, William," said Mallow. "I've come on urgent business. I must see Mr. Cabell at once. Can you please take me to him?"

Somehow, William kept his expression perfectly blank. "Mr. Cabell is in the study, sir. Please come this way."

"Never mind that, William, we know the way," said Mallow. He and his subordinates set off for the study. William followed, hoping none of the others would look back and see the grin of anticipatory enjoyment that he could no longer repress.

"Mr. Cabell?" said Mallow as he stepped into the study; but he found himself incapable of further speech or indeed movement. Sitting on the desk was Muirdyke, his left arm bare almost to the shoulder, bloodstained and bandaged. He held a glass of brandy in his good hand. Next to him sat Edwina, also holding a glass of brandy in one hand, and a large revolver in the other.

"Why, it's the Inspector!" exclaimed Edwina. "Hullo, Inspector," she added and raised her glass in greeting. After a moment, so did Charles.

Recovering from his temporary paralysis, Mallow stepped farther into the room and looked about to discover an opening in the wall where the French window had been, through which the storm was blowing. To the left of this was John Cabell, a bruise darkening his chin, lashed to the armchair. Casting about for something to say, he reverted to his early days as an ordinary constable and came out with, "What's all this, then?"

"If you've come about the murder, I'm afraid we've solved it," said Edwina, her voice not entirely steady. "There's the one," she continued, waving the revolver in the direction of the pinioned Cabell. "John Cabell, also known as Robert Callender." Suddenly the brandy, her overwrought nerves, and the expression on Mallow's face came together; she found herself laughing and crying uncontrollably and was obliged to bury her face in Charles's shoulder.

Mallow quickly stepped forward and took the revolver away from her. He turned to Cabell and began to ask, "Is this true?" — but his training caught up with him and instead he said, "Robert Callender, alias John Cabell, I arrest you on the charge of murdering the Honourable Mary Callender; and I warn you anything you say shall be taken down and may be used in evidence. Bellman, Pyke, release Cabell and take him out to the car. As for you two — I shall return tomorrow to hear your story."

Edwina recovered herself. "Don't forget to bring Pembert," she said.

"I'll bring him."

JUSTIS LIK TORTIS

Bringing Cabell back to headquarters and taking his statement took the rest of the night. At daybreak Mallow trudged through the wan morning light to his lodgings for a few hours' sleep. Waking at noon, he returned to made his report to Superintendent Runciman and arrange Pembert's release. Then, true to his word, he drove with the butler and Bellman to Minstrel Manor, arriving in the late afternoon. He was met at the door by William and ushered into the drawing room, where he found Charles resting comfortably on a sofa, and Edwina in a chair beside him, reading out loud one of his thrillers from the library, Roland Cole's *Killing in Kent*.

"Hullo, Inspector," said Edwina. "So you've come to hear our account of what happened last night?"

"Yes," said Mallow, "Bellman will take it down, but I don't think it will be necessary for official purposes. Oh, Pembert — please stay, as you were part of it."

So Edwina and Charles recounted to Mallow the events of the previous evening. Charles was inclined to understate his own involvement, but Edwina insisted on giving him full credit for her rescue. As the recital concluded, Mallow and Bellman, and even Pembert, joined in the laughter as Edwina described their reaction to the *tableau* in the study.

"And a good thing it won't be needed," said Mallow. "The trial will be sensational enough without adding a large helping of melodrama — although I daresay Mr. Oldfield would have appreciated it immensely."

"Do you have enough evidence without us?" asked Charles, a touch of disappointment in his voice.

"Oh, yes. Cabell — or rather, Robert Callender — knows we'll pin his wife's murder on him. He can't be hanged twice, so he's admitted he murdered Sebastian Oldfield as well."

"He talked?" asked Edwina.

"Talked? He wouldn't shut up. We had Pyke taking his statement, until he started to fall asleep, and then Porlock, until *he* got writer's cramp, and we had to bring in Bellman to finish. He'd had it all bottled up for fourteen years, unable to tell a soul, and it just came pouring out."

"He killed Uncle Sebastian over something that happened in 1913?" asked Charles.

"Mary Callender's murder?" added Edwina. "But that was 1912."

"Yes — and no," replied Mallow.

"How did he do it?" asked Charles.

Pembert open his mouth to speak, remembered he was only a servant, and closed it again.

"Go ahead, Pembert," said Charles. "We're all in this together."

"Well, sir," said Pembert. "When did he do it? It must have been just before I found Mr. Oldfield; but he was well on his way to London by then."

"The murder took place a little before 7:30," said Mallow.

"But I *saw* him leave at 7:00."

"Let's take things in order," said Mallow. "Cabell's story was that he had to start for Fenchester at seven because of the weather. In fact, he didn't have to leave that early. His car —"

"Had special tyres for snow," said Edwina.

"Yes," said Mallow, surprised. "How did you know?"

"He told me himself. And I never thought about it!"

"Why should you? Getting back to the story — the High Road curves around close to the rear of the manor. Cabell simply parked there and walked up. The window, like the door, can be opened from the outside as well as the inside. Cabell let himself in, and after the murder he left by the way he came. It would have been a weak alibi; but accidentally — with the assistance of your father, Miss Hackett — he turned it into a cast-iron one, or nearly so."

"Assistance from Dad? How?" asked Edwina.

"A great deal of snow came into the study with him. It would have melted by the time we got there, but the damp carpet would have given it away that the murderer came in by the window. When I spoke with Harry Bledsoe he mentioned that one of the things the shop was working on when Thomas Hackett was there was a climate-controller. Your father had a habit of 'improving' anything he was working on — he changed the controller so that it could be cranked up to a hundred and twenty degrees. Cabell didn't set it that high — just to a hundred — but by ten o'clock, the carpet was dry."

"But the study wasn't hot when Pembert and I got there," objected Edwina.

"Your father had also had the idea of combining a timer-switch with the climate-controller. Cabell set the switch to start the heat at 7:45 and run it until 9:45, then take the temperature down to fifty for ten minutes to cool the study, and finally to resume a normal setting of sixty-five just before ten."

"I don't follow," said Charles. "How did that help his alibi?"

"It kept Oldfield's body warm," replied Mallow. "Pembert noticed it. As a result, the post-mortem concluded the murder most likely took place shortly before ten, by which time Cabell was unimpeachably on the train to London."

"But that *is* cast-iron. Why did you say it was only *nearly* so?"

"Because there were contradictions in the post-mortem, so death just before ten o'clock was not a reliable conclusion. The heat hastened rigor, which indicated death may have taken place *before* seven. There were other, more technical signs that he had died around seven-thirty. And, of course, he was killed just after dining."

"And Cabell couldn't change the settings, because you'd taken his key away," said Edwina. "I wonder he didn't do so yesterday, after I returned it to him."

"He admitted that was carelessness on his part. He felt after Pembert's arrest there was no hurry."

"And so the heat came on again at 7:45 last night when I was trapped in the study," said Edwina. "Oh! That explains the butter!"

"Butter?" asked Charles.

"The butter that Mr. Oldfield spilled. I saw it the night he was killed, and again when we looked at the safe — it had run farther. And last night it had run farther still, dripping off the desk. Each night when the study was heated, the butter melted again."

"Ha!" exclaimed Charles. "A clue you had that the police didn't, Edwina. They should put you on the Force."

"Oh, I had a better one than that, Charles. I *knew* Mr. Oldfield had been killed well before ten."

"How did you know that?" asked Mallow.

"His blood was reddish brown, for one thing, not red. And the spilled wine was almost dry."

"Oh, good Lord!" exclaimed Mallow. "And *we* didn't realise it because we didn't see it until after two, when it looked perfectly natural… And I was so annoyed with you for going into the study that I never asked exactly what you'd seen."

"You *knew?* And you didn't say anything?" cried Pembert.

"I'm sorry, Pembert," replied Edwina. "I tried, but something always happened."

"There!" said Charles. "You *should* have Edwina on the Force."

Mallow grinned. "I doubt the Force would survive the experiment… It was a great shock to Cabell when you called and told him the study was hot."

"And a greater shock when I recognised him as Robert Callender. He came within an ace of shooting me."

"Once again, you were one up on us, Miss Hackett," said Mallow.

"But what put *you* on that trail?"

"How did we do it? I'll give it to you in order. Initially, you and Pembert appeared the most likely suspects, and also Mr. Muirdyke and Silas Painter, neither of whom had an alibi for the period from nine to ten. The first key came into our hands from Oldfield's bank, when we learned about the money he was paying Barnabas Merry-weather."

"Oh, him," said Charles. "I still can't get over that there really is a cove with that name. Where is he? Was he involved in all this?"

"Yes and no. The name and character of Merryweather were taken from *The Virtuous Villain* by someone else. When we opened Oldfield's safe we discovered who that someone was."

"Who?" asked Edwina.

"Oldfield himself."

"What?" exclaimed Edwina and Charles together.

"In his youth, Oldfield was an actor in a repertory company — we found playbills and newspaper clippings in the safe as well. 'Merry-weather' was one of the characters he portrayed.

"This, I confess, knocked me flat. So far as we could tell at first, someone had created the character of Merryweather in order to embezzle from Oldfield. But now we had Oldfield apparently embez-zling from himself.

"Meanwhile, we had also learned Robert Callender was somehow involved in the case, from the fact that the murderer had torn out from the volume of the *Panopticon* the issue recounting the murder of his wife, and the fact that Oldfield was unusually interested in that article.

"There was one more piece of evidence that turned out to be *the* key — the piece of the puzzle around which the others were arranged.

"This was a note found under Oldfield's body." Mallow showed them the words in his notebook: *justis lik tortis.*

"But that's from the play, isn't it?" said Charles. "How was it the key?"

"It's not the words, but the nature of the note. It was written by someone who couldn't spell; someone, in fact, who was completely illiterate."

"Who?" asked Charles.

"The note was written by Sebastian Oldfield."

"*What?*" said Charles again. Edwina was speechless.

"It's quite a story," said Mallow. "Some of it we deduced, but most of it came from Cabell himself. It started in 1912. At that time Oldfield was, and had been for several years, a successful actor, one of the principal players in the Holborn Repertory Company."

"But if he was illiterate, how did he learn his lines?" asked Edwina.

"Mr. Muirdyke actually answered that question days ago without knowing it. He said his uncle had memorised entire plays. Oldfield, in fact, had a phenomenal auditory memory: he could remember anything he had heard, word for word, even if he had only heard it once. All he had to do to learn a part was to have someone read the lines to him. We spoke yesterday with the manager of the company, who confirmed this. Incidentally, Cabell also mentioned his memory when we spoke with him the day after the murder, but misleadingly — he said Oldfield could remember anything he had *read.*

"As I was saying, Oldfield had been a successful actor. But he took to drink and in the summer of 1912 the company was compelled to dismiss him."

"Poor Uncle Sebastian," said Charles. "No wonder he was so down on *my* drinking."

"He had few acquaintances outside the theatrical profession. One of them was Robert Callender, a young man employed as a technician at the Wandsworth Glassworks in London. Callender had married the Honorable Mary Trevane — in the teeth of considerable parental opposition. The daughter of a wealthy peer, she was unable to accommodate her style of living to her husband's income. She ran up substantial debts; her father refused to help; she and Robert quarreled, and, as we know, late in 1912 he killed her. To avoid prison, and perhaps being hanged, he wrote a false suicide note and disappeared.

"What he did in fact was go to his friend Oldfield and tell a tale. He admitted the debts, but blamed himself, and said his wife had left him because of them. He had an invention he was sure would be a great success — an unbreakable glass — but needed capital to develop it, and couldn't do so under his own name because his creditors would seize it.

"He suggested Oldfield patent and develop the invention as his own, with Callender, under the name of John Cabell, acting as his assistant while managing everything behind the scenes. Oldfield, unemployed and, with his reputation as a drunkard, unemployable, jumped at the chance.

"Oldfield's Unbreakable Glass was indeed a great success, so much so that it almost ruined Callender's — or from that point on I should say Cabell's — plan. Oldfield suggested to Cabell that, with so much money coming in, he should be able to pay off his creditors and take his rightful place. He himself had overcome his drinking, at Cabell's insistence, and intended going back to his old profession."

"But surely the Callender murder was in the newspapers," said Edwina. "How could Mr. Oldfield not — oh, of course."

"Precisely. Cabell talked Oldfield out of it. He said his debts were far greater than he had at first admitted, so great they still couldn't be paid; and he enlarged on the awkward and embarrassing position Oldfield, now gaining prominence as an inventor, would be in if his imposture became known."

"But how could they have pulled it off in the first place?" asked Edwina. "If Mr. Oldfield was becoming a public figure, wouldn't it have become obvious he didn't have the knowledge to be what he claimed?"

"From the start, they played up Oldfield as a recluse who did his communicating through Cabell. Still, it was unavoidable that sometimes Oldfield would have to play his role in public and here his talents as an actor proved invaluable. At such times Cabell prepared Oldfield by providing him ahead of time with answers to likely questions. They also worked out a large repertoire of general statements and a system of cues. Cabell would be present, of course, and give Oldfield whatever cues he needed."

"Hold on," said Charles. "Wouldn't he have been afraid of being recognised as Callender?"

"At first he disguised himself," said Mallow. "Oldfield, of course, with his experience of stage make-up, was a great help to him. But he found it tedious and bothersome always to be doing this, and so he hit upon a more drastic method. He was a very stout young man; he concluded if he became a very thin one, no one could connect him with Callender.

"But we need to return to how Oldfield played his role as an inventor. The system worked well; but it broke down at least once, some years ago in Oldfield's workshop in Swannington."

"Oh!" exclaimed Edwina. "You mean the row with Dad?"

"Yes. Your father caught Oldfield away from Cabell and got him into a technical discussion. Oldfield was forced to *ad lib;* Thomas Hackett caught him out; and Oldfield had to cover up with a display of temper. Hackett responded in kind and got himself sacked. That was Cabell's doing — it was Oldfield who insisted on the letter of recommendation and the £250.

"Eventually Oldfield tired of the whole thing and wanted to get out, embarrassment or not. So Cabell blackmailed him: he told Oldfield — falsely — that he, Cabell, had perpetrated a number of questionable or even fraudulent deals and if they came out it would be Oldfield who went to prison.

"So Oldfield was driven to plan his own escape. He had three obstacles to overcome. The first was that he needed a new identity, as he still believed he could be prosecuted for fraud as Sebastian Oldfield. Fortunately, he had the persona of Merryweather ready to hand: he had kept much of his old theatrical paraphernalia, including costumes.

"The second was his illiteracy. He began teaching himself to read."

"Good Lord — by himself?" said Charles. "How on earth could he manage that?"

"Cabell did not say how, but I think we can make a reasonable conjecture. Pembert told me that, starting last summer, Oldfield began complaining of occasional migraines. He added the information that when one of these occurred, Oldfield dealt with it by lying in bed and having someone read to him. I suspect the migraines were a pretense. With his remarkable auditory memory he would remember, word for word, whatever had been read to him. Afterwards he could sit down and correlate what he heard with the printed text."

"But you said the note he left was the work of someone illiterate," said Edwina. "Why didn't it reflect that he could read?"

"Reading and writing are two different skills," replied Mallow. "Oldfield had learned to sign his name long ago, when he was an actor, but that was it. He had not taught himself to write before he was killed.

"Returning to our story, it was this — learning to read — which led to his undoing, and Cabell's. For one evening the reading was from the *Panopticon.* Oldfield now knew Mary Callender had not run away, but had been murdered, and Cabell, or Callender, had been lying to him from the beginning; and he alone knew Callender had not committed suicide. It now became an absolute necessity for him to escape."

"What was the third obstacle?" asked Edwina.

"Money, of course. Cabell held the purse strings. He had no objection to indulging Oldfield with anything he wanted — a model railway, the allowance to his nephew, even Minstrel Manor itself — for he didn't really care about the money coming in. He was concerned first with his own safety and after that with his work. But he never allowed Oldfield a penny of actual cash.

"Oldfield's first move was impulsive. Cabell had been receiving, through the post, small quantities of gold for use in his work. Oldfield managed to intercept one of these, but then Cabell began going to London to fetch them himself. He wouldn't have got far with it in any event — the gold was only worth a few pounds.

"Oldfield then realised he needed to plan carefully. He knew that, although Cabell controlled the money, it was still in his — Oldfield's — name, so Cabell signed cheques as 'Sebastian Oldfield'. He practised until he was able to forge the signature fairly well."

"Why didn't he ask me?" said Pembert. "He knew my past. I'd have done anything to help him."

"You were recommended by Howard Draven to Cabell — Oldfield may not have been completely certain of your loyalty. Also — this is my conjecture only — he respected your desire to keep straight too much to involve you in such a dubious business.

"When he had mastered the forgery, he was ready to begin. He got Pembert to write a letter introducing Barnabas Merryweather to a bank in Chiltonbury — so you see, Pembert, you helped him after all — and armed with this opened an account. This done, whenever Cabell was absent on business, he wrote a cheque and had Pembert drive him to Chiltonbury, where he had engaged a hotel room as Merryweather. There he disguised himself and deposited the money. By instructing the staff of the manor to route all communications from either bank to himself, he was able to keep knowledge of the transactions from Cabell.

"At the same time he was able briefly to enjoy some ordinary human fellowship by visiting the Green Wyvern in his role as Merry-weather. There he made the acquaintance of Silas Painter. It had, of course, been Cabell who had taken Painter's farm, but he had had to work through Oldfield, who had insisted on a pension and a house in the village. He had not known how much Painter resented what had been done to him, and so promised him he should be righted. I suppose that's up to you now, Mr. Muirdyke."

"He *shan't* get the land back," said Charles. "He has no right to it; he wasn't doing anything with it; and I'll wager ten quid to a farthing he's happier with a warm house, all the beer he can drink, and a grievance to nurse."

"Returning to Oldfield," continued Mallow. "The one flaw in his plan was that Cabell might discover the money going out before he could escape. Unfortunately for him, Cabell did discover it. On the morning of the murder he had gone to Oldfield's bank in Swannington on a matter of business. While there he discovered Oldfield's account was six thousand pounds short. From further inquiry he learned of the payments to 'Merryweather.' That name pointed directly to Oldfield — remember, Cabell had known him when he was acting. Cabell returned to the manor —"

"And murdered Uncle Sebastian," said Charles.

"No. At least, not then. They argued, but Oldfield stuck to his determination to escape; in fact, he said, he'd made up his mind to leave as soon as Miss Hackett had finished his portrait."

"But if Cabell knew Uncle Sebastian could expose him as Callender, why didn't he kill him then?" asked Charles.

"He didn't know it — then. Oldfield kept that knowledge to himself. But Cabell returned to the study. Once again he threatened Oldfield with prison; Oldfield countered by threatening *him* with hanging. He revealed that he knew of the article in the *Panopticon*. Cabell, realising he was in mortal danger, picked up the paperweight and struck. At least, that's his story. He may have had murder at the back of his mind all along. Setting up an alibi suggests premeditation."

"But how did you work it out?" asked Edwina.

"As we were looking at the evidence, the key question came to me," replied Mallow. "*Suppose Oldfield* had *written the note? That he was* not *the great inventor he seemed to be?* If so, who but Cabell could be, and always had been, the real brain behind him? The article mentioned that Robert Callender was employed at a glassworks; Oldfield's first invention was an unbreakable glass. There was then at least a strong probability John Cabell and Robert Callender were one and the same. The Callender file at the Yard made it certain. The handwriting of the suicide note was Cabell's; and to make assurance doubly sure —"

"Macbeth," murmured Bellman. "Misquoted, as always."

"— The Yard had searched the Callender flat after Mary Callender's murder, and, of course, had found Robert's fingerprints. They kept these in the file in case they should be needed to identify Robert's body if in fact he *had* committed suicide. The fingerprints matched those of John Cabell."

"But you had Cabell's fingerprints on Tuesday," said Charles. "Why didn't you take them to the Yard then?"

"We did. But Robert Callender had never been arrested. His prints were not on file as a criminal." Mallow rose. "I must take my leave now. There's a great deal still to be done —"

"Aha!" exclaimed Charles. "It's just like in the thrillers. The murderer made a fatal error!"

"What was it?" asked Mallow.

"If he had taken the entire bound volume, instead of tearing out that one issue, you'd never have known that Callender was involved at all."

Mallow blinked and sat down again. After a moment he said, "Do you know — that hadn't occurred to me." He rose again. "Goodbye, Miss Hackett — Mr. Muirdyke — Pembert. I hope your arm isn't too bad, Mr. Muirdyke?"

"Uncle Sebastian's physician came this morning and looked at it," replied Charles. "He said my arm should be O.K."

"Glad to hear it. Oh — I had almost forgot. Cabell wants you to go to the workshop, Mr. Muirdyke — he is very concerned about the animals: they must be fed and their cages cleaned. Here are his keys. He also wants you to see about getting someone to take over his work; he suggested you consult Howard Draven."

"The blighter puts a hole in me and then expects me to run errands for him?" exclaimed Charles. "I'm dashed if I'll do it!"

"Now, Charles, think," said Edwina. "We don't want innocent animals to suffer, do we? And whatever Cabell was working on could very well be valuable. Look — I'll come along and help."

"Oh, all right," grudged Charles.

"Goodbye, Miss Hackett," said Mallow.

"Goodbye, Inspector. It's been quite a week, hasn't it?"

"It has. I hope you've come to realise a murder investigation is not a game."

"Of course it isn't," replied Edwina with a smile. "But it *is* an adventure."

SHE TURNED A CORNER AND WAS LOST TO SIGHT

Taking care of the rabbits, guinea pigs, rats, and mice — and the snake — in the workshop took the rest of Saturday afternoon. Charles, pleading his injured arm, left most of the work to Edwina while he wandered about, looking in drawers, poking about in Cabell's papers, and laughing at Oldfield's cartoons of Cabell. He showed Edwina the one of Oldfield himself that Mallow had seen.

Edwina, her arms full of clean litter, glanced at it. "I don't understand it," she replied.

"I think I do. It's Uncle Sebastian, mocking himself."

"Mocking himself?"

"He was supposed to be a great inventor; but he's drawn himself as a little man, standing on Cabell's shoulders; Cabell, who stays in the shadows and does all the work."

Edwina was taken aback. She had not expected Charles to be capable of this level of insight. "I see it now," she said. "The poor man. Spending all those years as someone else's puppet... I wonder what Cabell would have done if he had got away with it."

"Carried on, I suppose, claiming he was finishing my uncle's work. I have to say, the old boy was dashed clever — first to put over the act, and then think of how to get out of it. I wonder what *he* would have done."

"Probably got a job as an actor again. Look, Charles, if you're going to mooch about, see if you can find some shellac."

"What for?"

"My sketches."

Edwina arose early Sunday morning to pack her clothes and painting gear. The shellac (Charles had found some) on the sketches was dry; she carefully wrapped Cabell's, intending to stop in Fenchester on her way home and, if allowed, to give it to him.

Charles did not come to breakfast. Edwina considered retrieving *War and Peace* from her baggage but decided it was too much trouble; she settled in the library with one of Charles's thrillers instead. She had just reached the second murder when she heard the church bell in Minstrel Folly ringing.

Edwina was not a regular church-goer; but on impulse she got her car and drove down to attend the morning service. Providence had brought Charles on to the scene Friday night to rescue her; it was only proper to give thanks.

Returning after the service she found Charles still not up. While William carried her impedimenta out to her car, she sat down in the hall and scribbled a farewell note. Just as she was putting it into an envelope, Charles came galloping down the stairs, garbed in a kelly-green bathrobe over bright orange pyjamas.

"I say, Edwina," he gasped as he reached the bottom, "I'm dashed sorry — overslept and all that. Didn't want you to leave without a proper goodbye, you know."

"Well — goodbye, then," said Edwina, holding out her hand. Charles took it in both of his, rather awkwardly as his left arm was still in its sling.

"I say, it was jolly fun, you being here — bags of excitement," he said. "I'll be living here now — dashed odd, me being lord of the manor — anyhow, if you ever want to pay another visit, you'd be more than welcome."

"Thank you, Charles," said Edwina. "I think I should like to return sometime." Removing her hand from his, she went on, "By the way, I left your portrait in the library."

"Thanks," said Charles. "I'll keep it with me — reminder that I ought to make something of myself and all that."

"I'm sure you will," said Edwina. "And now I really must be going." Charles accompanied her out the door. She got into her car and drove off. Charles stood watching until she turned a corner and was lost to sight.

Friday's storm had been followed by a thaw and the roads were deep in slush. By the time Edwina arrived in Fenchester, her Abbey was coated with the stains of mud and the grey sludge of the town's streets. She parked outside police headquarters, took the sketch of Cabell, and went in and asked to see Inspector Mallow.

"Miss Hackett!" exclaimed Mallow, emerging from his office. "This is a pleasant surprise. What can I do for you?"

"First, I'd like to speak with Mr. Cabell, if I may," replied Edwina, "and to give him this." She unwrapped the sketch and showed it to Mallow. "I promised him he should have it."

"I'll take it to him and tell him you're here," said Mallow. Taking the sketch, he set off for the rear of the building, where the gaol was located.

A few minutes later he returned, still carrying the sketch. "I'm very sorry," he said, "but Cabell doesn't want it, and doesn't want to see you either. I'm afraid he was rather bitter about it. You see, you were the one who saw through his disguise and then made a fool of him. He's not the sort of man who takes humiliation easily."

"Oh, dear," said Edwina. "I'll keep the sketch for him, should he ever change his mind."

Unlikely, thought Mallow. *He'll be hanged before Spring arrives.*

"By the way," continued Edwina, "I forgot to congratulate you yesterday for solving the case so quickly — despite me."

"Thank you — but I *didn't* solve the case, if you mean Oldfield's murder. I solved the Callender murder — and *that,* as Charles Muirdyke pointed out, was a fluke. If Cabell hadn't confessed, I don't know we should ever have brought it home to him."

"But you had plenty of evidence. There was the climate-controller, and the tyres for snow, and the button that opened the French window, and the whole Merryweather business."

"Circumstantial evidence only. Enough that we should have been morally certain of his guilt, but not necessarily enough to convince a jury."

"Especially a Fenshire jury," said Edwina, still bitter about the inquest.

"Yes, I should apologise for that. I mishandled the inquest dreadfully — as Superintendent Runciman was kind enough to point out."

"It *was* your first case, after all. You should have heard what the instructor said when I showed him my first painting. If I hadn't been so sure of what I wanted to do, I'd have chucked the whole business." Edwina laughed. "I might have joined the police, after all."

"That would have meant a great loss for Art — and I don't dare contemplate what it would have meant for the police... May I walk you to your car?" asked Mallow.

"Of course."

Mallow escorted Edwina out of police headquarters. As they came to the car, he cleared his throat, paused, and said, "I wish we had met in other circumstances, Miss Hackett. I should have liked to improve our acquaintance."

"Why should the circumstances matter?" replied Edwina. "I didn't find them objectionable — that is, I should have preferred — that is, it would have been better had Mr. Oldfield not been murdered —"

"Well, then," said Mallow, "may I call on you sometime — or perhaps take you out to dinner?"

"I should like that very much, Inspector," said Edwina. She looked at the Abbey. "It's going to be a job and a half getting that clean," she remarked. Turning back to Mallow she added, "But don't propose."

"Why would I do that?"

For some reason Edwina found this instant negative disappointing. "I don't know," she replied after a moment. "Everybody else does. But I really must go. I'm overdue for a commission in Rutlandshire." She got into her car and drove off. Mallow stood watching until she turned a corner and was lost to sight.

ACKNOWLEDGMENTS

Many thanks to Richard Rosinski, Rich Breen, Ginny Shepard, Mitzi Flyte, and especially Nick Hamlyn for their comments.

And thanks to Laurel, Beth, and Rebecca for listening while I talked through problems with the plot.

ABOUT THE AUTHOR

Robert Wenson spent 20 years as a draftsman / structural designer / civil engineer and another 22 as a computer programmer. In his off hours he did a fair amount of scribbling for his own amusement and that of others. He retired in 2020 to concentrate on writing full-time. He lives in Bethlehem, PA with his wife of over thirty years and their two children. And a cat.